Praise for the Novels of
#1 *New York Times* Bestselling Author
Nicholas Sparks

Every Breath

"Sparks is known for crafting sweeping romances that make readers feel deeply and believe in the power of love...Sparks confirms his gifts...in this thoughtfully researched and spellbinding story of love that defies time, a tale both heartbreaking and heartwarming."
—*Booklist*

"What makes *Every Breath* rise above...is its unpredictability and strong character development."
—*USA Today*

"A heart-wrenching tale of fate and circumstance...an epic romance...Sparks fans will not be disappointed."
—*Publishers Weekly*

Two by Two

"Sparks invites readers to take a journey that stares risks and rewards directly in the face. Whether it's tenderness between a husband and wife or affection between a father and his daughter, Sparks has definitely mastered the art of love."
—*The Washington Times*

"Nicholas Sparks creates magic once again with [this] latest emotionally powerful novel."

—*RT Book Reviews*

See Me

"Sparks takes readers on a roller-coaster ride of emotion, from the soft tone of a love story to the adrenaline rush of a thriller." —Associated Press

"*See Me* is not only a tender, engaging, and heartwarming story, but it displays the meshing of two different and opposite lives that come together to prove that love conquers all. Gripping and riveting suspense adds another layer of depth and interest."

—*New York Journal of Books*

"Powerful proof that Nicholas Sparks is a masterful storyteller who remains at the top of his game."

—BookReporter.com

"This deeply emotional book once again proves that Sparks understands human nature and relationships as well as anyone writing today."

—BarnesandNoble.com

The Longest Ride

"Sparks is a poet...a master." —*Philadelphia Inquirer*

"*The Longest Ride* is epic Sparks...[It] showcases the author's most accomplished work to date...There are moments of perfection...Reaching not only young and old, the novel is commingled with enough cowboy action, literary flavor, and a maturing gift for dialogue to reach across the sexes."

—*Mountain Times* (NC)

The Best of Me

"A creative genius...his book is great for any love story enthusiast."   —HubPages.com

"Unforgettable...Makes you settle in for another romantic date with this well-respected and talented storyteller."

—*Fredericksburg Free Lance-Star* (VA)

"I could not put it down...a classic Nicholas Sparks tragedy but with a twist of hope...If I can pick my favorites from him, *The Best of Me* will rank with *Message in a Bottle* and *The Notebook*—it was *that* good."

—BookReporter.com

Safe Haven

"A compelling love story...a gripping tale of love and survival...a riveting 'read all night' page-turner."

—BookReporter.com

"Sparks has written another wonderful love story that makes you see true love in its simplest form and believe in it...a fantastic book about relationships, love, trust, and friendships." —BestsellersWorld.com

The Last Song

"Romance, betrayal, and youthful discovery...Fans of *The Notebook, Message in a Bottle*, etc., will gobble it up." —*Entertainment Weekly*

"A very enjoyable read...a plot that allows his characters to learn and grow from their experiences...Sparks is at his best." —*Greensboro News-Record* (NC)

"Raw emotion, young love, family angst, and—ultimately—sweet resolution." —*BookPage*

The Lucky One

"A tale of redemption...holds readers in suspense until the final chapter...it will test readers' beliefs in the power of destiny and fate, and how they relate to choices one makes in life." —*Chattanooga Times Free Press*

"In true Nicholas Sparks fashion, the reader is engaged from the first to last page. The characters are authentic and the plot is engrossing and emotionally charged." —BookLoons.com

The Choice

"A tender and moving love story."
—*Publishers Weekly*

"A heartrending love story...will have you entranced. And if *The Notebook* left you teary-eyed, his latest will have the same effect."
—*Myrtle Beach Sun News*

Dear John

"Beautifully moving...Has tremendous emotional depth, revealing the true meaning of unconditional love."
—*RT Book Reviews*

"For Sparks, weighty matters of the day remain set pieces, furniture upon which to hang timeless tales of chaste longing and harsh fate."
—*Washington Post Book World*

"Sparks lives up to his reputation...a tribute to courageous and self-sacrificing soldiers."
—*Booklist*

At First Sight

"An ending that surprises."
—*New York Times Book Review*

"Nicholas Sparks is one of the best-known writers in America and overseas for good reason: He has written stories that reveal the yearning for our most prized possession: love."
—*Mobile Register* (AL)

True Believer

"Time for a date with Sparks...The slow dance to the couple's first kiss is a two-chapter guilty pleasure."
—*People*

"Another winner...a page-turner...has all the things we have come to expect from him: sweet romance and a strong sense of place."
—*Charlotte Observer*

The Wedding

"Sweet but packs a punch...There is a twist that pulls everything together and makes you glad you read this."
—*Charlotte Observer*

"Sparks tells his sweet story...[with] a gasp-inducing twist at the very end. Satisfied female readers will close the covers with a sigh."
—*Publishers Weekly*

The Guardian

"An involving love story...an edge-of-your-seat, unpredictable thriller."
—*Booklist*

"Nicholas Sparks is a top-notch writer. He has created a truly spine-tingling thriller exploring love and obsession with a kind of suspense never before experienced in his novels."   —RedBank.com

Nights in Rodanthe

"Bittersweet...romance blooms...You'll cry in spite of yourself."   —*People*

"Passionate and memorable...smooth, sensitive writing...This is a novel that can hold its own."
—Associated Press

"Extremely hard to put down...a love story, and a good love story at that."   —*Boston Herald*

A Bend in the Road

"Sweet, accessible, uplifting."   —*Publishers Weekly*

"A powerful tale of true love."   —*Booklist*

The Rescue

"A romantic page-turner...Sparks's fans won't be disappointed."   —*Glamour*

"All of Sparks's trademark elements—love, loss, and small-town life—are present in this terrific read."
—*Booklist*

A Walk to Remember

"An extraordinary book...touching, at times riveting...a book you won't soon forget."
—*New York Post*

"A sweet tale of young but everlasting love."
—*Chicago Sun-Times*

"Bittersweet...a tragic yet spiritual love story."
—*Variety*

Message in a Bottle

"The novel's unabashed emotion—and an unexpected turn—will put tears in your eyes."
—*People*

"Glows with moments of tenderness...delve[s] deeply into the mysteries of eternal love."
—*Cleveland Plain Dealer*

"Deeply moving, beautifully written, and extremely romantic."
—*Booklist*

The Notebook

"Nicholas Sparks...will not let you go. His novel shines."   —*Dallas Morning News*

"Proves that good things come in small packages...a classic tale of love."   —*Christian Science Monitor*

"The lyrical beauty of this touching love story...will captivate the heart of every reader and establish Nicholas Sparks as a gifted novelist."
                    —*Denver Rocky Mountain News*

Also by Nicholas Sparks

Every Breath
Two by Two
See Me
The Longest Ride
The Best of Me
Safe Haven
The Last Song
The Lucky One
The Choice
Dear John
At First Sight
True Believer
Three Weeks with My Brother
The Wedding
The Guardian
Nights in Rodanthe
A Bend in the Road
The Rescue
A Walk to Remember
Message in a Bottle
The Notebook

NICHOLAS SPARKS

A WALK TO REMEMBER

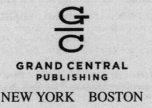

GRAND CENTRAL
PUBLISHING

NEW YORK   BOSTON

Copyright © 1999 by Nicholas Sparks Enterprises, Inc.
Excerpt from *Every Breath* copyright © 2018 by Willow Holdings, Inc.

Cover design by Anna Dorfman; hand-lettering by Nick Misani

Grand Central Publishing
Hachette Book Group
1290 Avenue of the Americas, New York, NY 10104
grandcentralpublishing.com
twitter.com/grandcentralpub

Originally published in hardcover in October 1999
First mass market edition: September 2000
Reissued: December 2001, November 2019

Grand Central Publishing is a division of Hachette Book Group, Inc. The Grand Central Publishing name and logo is a trademark of Hachette Book Group, Inc.

The publisher is not responsible for websites (or their content) that are not owned by the publisher.

The Hachette Speakers Bureau provides a wide range of authors for speaking events. To find out more, go to hachettespeakersbureau.com or call (866) 376-6591.

ISBNs: 978-1-5387-6470-1 (mass market reissue), 978-0-7595-2026-4 (ebook)

Printed in the United States of America

OPM

10 9 8 7 6 5 4 3 2 1

For my parents, with love and memories.

Patrick Michael Sparks (1942–1996)
Jill Emma Marie Sparks (1942–1989)

And for my siblings, with all my heart and soul.

Micah Sparks
Danielle Lewis

Prologue

⌒

When I was seventeen, my life changed forever.

I know that there are people who wonder about me when I say this. They look at me strangely as if trying to fathom what could have happened back then, though I seldom bother to explain. Because I've lived here for most of my life, I don't feel that I have to unless it's on my terms, and that would take more time than most people are willing to give me. My story can't be summed up in two or three sentences; it can't be packaged into something neat and simple that people would immediately understand. Despite the passage of forty years, the people still living here who knew me that year accept my lack of explanation without question. My story in some ways is their story because it was something that all of us lived through.

It was I, however, who was closest to it.

I'm fifty-seven years old, but even now I can remember everything from that year, down to the smallest details. I relive that year often in my mind, bringing it back to life, and I realize that when I do, I always feel a strange combination of sadness and joy. There are moments when I wish I could roll back the clock and take all the sadness away, but I have the feeling that if I did, the joy would be gone as well. So I take the memories as they come, accepting them all, letting them guide me whenever I can. This happens more often than I let on.

It is April 12, in the last year before the millennium, and as I leave my house, I glance around. The sky is overcast and gray, but as I move down the street, I notice that the dogwoods and azaleas are blooming. I zip my jacket just a little. The temperature is cool, though I know it's only a matter of weeks before it will settle in to something comfortable and the gray skies give way to the kind of days that make North Carolina one of the most beautiful places in the world.

With a sigh, I feel it all coming back to me. I close my eyes and the years begin to move in reverse, slowly ticking backward, like the hands of a clock rotating in the wrong direction. As if through someone else's eyes, I watch myself grow younger; I see my hair changing from gray to brown, I feel the wrinkles around my eyes begin to smooth, my arms and legs grow sinewy. Lessons I've learned with age grow dimmer, and my innocence returns as that eventful year approaches.

Then, like me, the world begins to change: roads narrow and some become gravel, suburban sprawl has been replaced with farmland, downtown streets teem with people, looking in windows as they pass Sweeney's bakery and Palka's meat shop. Men wear hats, women wear dresses. At the courthouse up the street, the bell tower rings....

I open my eyes and pause. I am standing outside the Baptist church, and when I stare at the gable, I know exactly who I am.

My name is Landon Carter, and I'm seventeen years old.

This is my story; I promise to leave nothing out.

First you will smile, and then you will cry—don't say you haven't been warned.

One

In 1958, Beaufort, North Carolina, which is located on the coast near Morehead City, was a place like many other small southern towns. It was the kind of place where the humidity rose so high in the summer that walking out to get the mail made a person feel as if he needed a shower, and kids walked around barefoot from April through October beneath oak trees draped in Spanish moss. People waved from their cars whenever they saw someone on the street whether they knew him or not, and the air smelled of pine, salt, and sea, a scent unique to the Carolinas. For many of the people there, fishing in the Pamlico Sound or crabbing in the Neuse River was a way of life, and boats were moored wherever you saw the Intracoastal Waterway. Only three channels came in on the television, though television was never important to those of us who grew up there. Instead our lives were centered around the churches, of which there were eighteen within the town limits alone. They went by names like the Fellowship

Hall Christian Church, the Church of the Forgiven People, the Church of Sunday Atonement, and then, of course, there were the Baptist churches. When I was growing up, it was far and away the most popular denomination around, and there were Baptist churches on practically every corner of town, though each considered itself superior to the others. There were Baptist churches of every type—Freewill Baptists, Southern Baptists, Congregational Baptists, Missionary Baptists, Independent Baptists...well, you get the picture.

Back then, the big event of the year was sponsored by the Baptist church downtown—Southern, if you really want to know—in conjunction with the local high school. Every year they put on their Christmas pageant at the Beaufort Playhouse, which was actually a play that had been written by Hegbert Sullivan, a minister who'd been with the church since Moses parted the Red Sea. Okay, maybe he wasn't that old, but he was old enough that you could almost see through the guy's skin. It was sort of clammy all the time, and translucent—kids would swear they actually saw the blood flowing through his veins—and his hair was as white as those bunnies you see in pet stores around Easter.

Anyway, he wrote this play called *The Christmas Angel*, because he didn't want to keep on performing that old Charles Dickens classic *A Christmas Carol*. In his mind Scrooge was a heathen, who came to his redemption only because he saw ghosts, not angels—and who was to say whether they'd been sent by God, anyway? And who was to say he wouldn't revert to his sinful ways if they hadn't been sent directly from

heaven? The play didn't exactly tell you in the end—
it sort of plays into faith and all—but Hegbert didn't
trust ghosts if they weren't actually sent by God, which
wasn't explained in plain language, and this was his
big problem with it. A few years back he'd changed the
end of the play—sort of followed it up with his own
version, complete with old man Scrooge becoming a
preacher and all, heading off to Jerusalem to find the
place where Jesus once taught the scribes. It didn't fly
too well—not even to the congregation, who sat in the
audience staring wide-eyed at the spectacle—and the
newspaper said things like "Though it was certainly
interesting, it wasn't exactly the play we've all come to
know and love..."

So Hegbert decided to try his hand at writing his
own play. He'd written his own sermons his whole
life, and some of them, we had to admit, were actually
interesting, especially when he talked about the "wrath
of God coming down on the fornicators" and all that
good stuff. That really got his blood boiling, I'll tell
you, when he talked about the fornicators. That was
his real hot spot. When we were younger, my friends
and I would hide behind the trees and shout, "Hegbert
is a fornicator!" when we saw him walking down the
street, and we'd giggle like idiots, like we were the wit-
tiest creatures ever to inhabit the planet.

Old Hegbert, he'd stop dead in his tracks and his
ears would perk up—I swear to God, they actually
moved—and he'd turn this bright shade of red, like
he'd just drunk gasoline, and the big green veins in
his neck would start sticking out all over, like those
maps of the Amazon River that you see in *National*

Geographic. He'd peer from side to side, his eyes narrowing into slits as he searched for us, and then, just as suddenly, he'd start to go pale again, back to that fishy skin, right before our eyes. Boy, it was something to watch, that's for sure.

So we'd be hiding behind a tree and Hegbert (what kind of parents name their kid Hegbert, anyway?) would stand there waiting for us to give ourselves up, as if he thought we'd be that stupid. We'd put our hands over our mouths to keep from laughing out loud, but somehow he'd always zero in on us. He'd be turning from side to side, and then he'd stop, those beady eyes coming right at us, right through the tree. "I know who you are, Landon Carter," he'd say, "and the Lord knows, too." He'd let that sink in for a minute or so, and then he'd finally head off again, and during the sermon that weekend he'd stare right at us and say something like "God is merciful to children, but the children must be worthy as well." And we'd sort of lower ourselves in the seats, not from embarrassment, but to hide a new round of giggles. Hegbert didn't understand us at all, which was really sort of strange, being that he had a kid and all. But then again, she was a girl. More on that, though, later.

Anyway, like I said, Hegbert wrote *The Christmas Angel* one year and decided to put on *that* play instead. The play itself wasn't bad, actually, which surprised everyone the first year it was performed. It's basically the story of a man who had lost his wife a few years back. This guy, Tom Thornton, used to be real religious, but he had a crisis of faith after his wife died during childbirth. He's raising this little girl all on his own, but he hasn't been the greatest father, and what the little girl really wants for Christmas is a special music box with an angel engraved on top, a picture of which she'd cut out from an old catalog. The guy searches long and hard to find the gift, but he can't find it anywhere. So it's Christmas Eve and he's still searching, and while he's out looking through the stores, he comes across a strange woman he's never seen before, and she promises to help him find the gift for his daughter. First, though, they help this homeless person (back then they were called bums, by the way), then they stop at an orphanage to see some kids, then visit a lonely old woman who just wanted some company on Christmas Eve. At this point the mysterious woman asks Tom Thornton what he wants for Christmas, and he says that he wants his wife back. She brings him to the city fountain and tells him to look in the water and he'll find what he's looking for. When he looks in the water, he sees the face of his little girl, and he breaks down and cries right there. While he's sobbing, the mysterious lady runs off, and Tom Thornton searches but can't find her anywhere. Eventually he heads home, the lessons from the evening playing in his mind. He walks into his little girl's room, and her sleeping figure makes him realize that she's all he has left of his wife, and he starts to cry again because he knows he hasn't been a good enough father to her. The next morning, magically, the music box is underneath the tree, and the angel that's engraved on it looks exactly like the woman he'd seen the night before.

So it wasn't that bad, really. If truth be told, people cried buckets whenever they saw it. The play sold out every year it was performed, and due to its popularity, Hegbert eventually had to move it from the church to the Beaufort Playhouse, which had a lot more seating. By the time I was a senior in high school, the performances ran twice to packed houses, which, considering who actually performed it, was a story in and of itself.

You see, Hegbert wanted young people to perform the play—seniors in high school, not the theater group. I reckon he thought it would be a good learning experience before the seniors headed off to college and came face-to-face with all the fornicators. He was that kind of guy, you know, always wanting to save us from temptation. He wanted us to know that God is out there watching you, even when you're away from home, and that if you put your trust in God, you'll be all right in the end. It was a lesson that I would eventually learn in time, though it wasn't Hegbert who taught me.

As I said before, Beaufort was fairly typical as far as southern towns went, though it did have an interesting history. Blackbeard the pirate once owned a house there, and his ship, *Queen Anne's Revenge*, is supposedly buried somewhere in the sand just offshore. Recently some archaeologists or oceanographers or whoever looks for stuff like that said they found it, but no one's certain just yet, being that it sank over 250 years ago and you can't exactly reach into the glove compartment and check the registration. Beaufort's come a long way since the 1950s, but it's still not exactly a major metropolis or anything. Beaufort was, and always will be, on the smallish side, but when I was growing up, it barely warranted a place on the map. To put it into perspective, the congressional district that included Beaufort covered the entire eastern part of the state—some twenty thousand square miles—and there wasn't a single town with more than twenty-five thousand people. Even compared with those towns, Beaufort was regarded as being on the small side. Everything east of Raleigh and north of Wilmington, all the way to the Virginia border, was the district my father represented.

I suppose you've heard of him. He's sort of a legend, even now. His name is Worth Carter, and he was a congressman for almost thirty years. His slogan every other year during the election season was "Worth Carter represents————," and the person was supposed to fill in the city name where he or she lived. I can remember, driving on trips when me and Mom had to make our appearances to show the people he was a true family man, that we'd see those bumper stickers, stenciled in with names like Otway and Chocowinity and Seven Springs. Nowadays stuff like that wouldn't fly, but back then that was fairly sophisticated publicity. I imagine if he tried to do that now, people opposing him would insert all sorts of foul language in the blank space, but we never saw it once. Okay, maybe once. A farmer from Duplin County once wrote the word *shit* in the blank space, and when my mom saw it, she covered my eyes and said a prayer asking for forgiveness for the poor ignorant bastard. She didn't say exactly those words, but I got the gist of it.

So my father, Mr. Congressman, was a bigwig, and everyone but everyone knew it, including old man

Hegbert. Now, the two of them didn't get along, not at
all, despite the fact that my father went to Hegbert's
church whenever he was in town, which to be frank
wasn't all that often. Hegbert, in addition to his belief
that fornicators were destined to clean the urinals in
hell, also believed that communism was "a sickness
that doomed mankind to heathenhood." Even though
heathenhood wasn't a word—I can't find it in any
dictionary—the congregation knew what he meant.
They also knew that he was directing his words specifically to my father, who would sit with his eyes closed
and pretend not to listen. My father was on one of the
House committees that oversaw the "Red influence"
supposedly infiltrating every aspect of the country,
including national defense, higher education, and even
tobacco farming. You have to remember that this was
during the cold war; tensions were running high, and
we North Carolinians needed something to bring it
down to a more personal level. My father had consis-
tently looked for facts, which were irrelevant to people
like Hegbert.

Afterward, when my father would come home after
the service, he'd say something like "Reverend Sullivan was in rare form today. I hope you heard that part
about the Scripture where Jesus was talking about the
poor...."

Yeah, sure, Dad....

My father tried to defuse situations whenever possible. I think that's why he stayed in Congress for so
long. The guy could kiss the ugliest babies known to
mankind and still come up with something nice to say.
"He's such a gentle child," he'd say when a baby had

a giant head, or, "I'll bet she's the sweetest girl in the world," if she had a birthmark over her entire face. One time a lady showed up with a kid in a wheelchair. My father took one look at him and said, "I'll bet you ten to one that you're the smartest kid in your class." And he was! Yeah, my father was great at stuff like that. He could fling it with the best of 'em, that's for sure. And he wasn't such a bad guy, not really, especially if you consider the fact that he didn't beat me or anything.

But he wasn't there for me growing up. I hate to say that because nowadays people claim that sort of stuff even if their parent *was* around and use it to excuse their behavior. *My dad...he didn't love me...that's why I became a stripper and performed on* The Jerry Springer Show.... I'm not using it to excuse the person I've become, I'm simply saying it as a fact. My father was gone nine months of the year, living out of town in a Washington, D.C., apartment three hundred miles away. My mother didn't go with him because both of them wanted me to grow up "the same way they had."

Of course, my father's father took him hunting and fishing, taught him to play ball, showed up for birthday parties, all that small stuff that adds up to quite a bit before adulthood. My father, on the other hand, was a stranger, someone I barely knew at all. For the first five years of my life I thought all fathers lived somewhere else. It wasn't until my best friend, Eric Hunter, asked me in kindergarten who that guy was who showed up at my house the night before that I realized something wasn't quite right about the situation.

"He's my father," I said proudly.

"Oh," Eric said as he rifled through my lunch-box,

looking for my Milky Way, "I didn't know you had a father."

Talk about something whacking you straight in the face.

So, I grew up under the care of my mother. Now she was a nice lady, sweet and gentle, the kind of mother most people dream about. But she wasn't, nor could she ever be, a manly influence in my life, and that fact, coupled with my growing disillusionment with my father, made me become something of a rebel, even at a young age. Not a bad one, mind you. Me and my friends might sneak out late and soap up car windows now and then or eat boiled peanuts in the graveyard behind the church, but in the fifties that was the kind of thing that made other parents shake their heads and whisper to their children, "You don't want to be like that Carter boy. He's on the fast track to prison."

Me. A bad boy. For eating boiled peanuts in the graveyard. Go figure.

Anyway, my father and Hegbert didn't get along, but it wasn't only because of politics. No, it seems that my father and Hegbert knew each other from way back when. Hegbert was about twenty years older than my father, and back before he was a minister, he used to work for my father's father. My grandfather—even though he spent lots of time with my father—was a true bastard if there ever was one. He was the one, by the way, who made the family fortune, but I don't want you to imagine him as the sort of man who slaved over his business, working diligently and watching it grow, prospering slowly over time. My grandfather was much shrewder than that. The way he made his money was simple—he started as a bootlegger, accumulating wealth throughout Prohibition by running rum up from Cuba. Then he began buying land and hiring sharecroppers to work it. He took ninety percent of the money the sharecroppers made on their tobacco crop, then loaned them money whenever they needed it at ridiculous interest rates. Of course, he never intended to collect the money—instead he would foreclose on any land or equipment they happened to own. Then, in what he called "his moment of inspiration," he started a bank called Carter Banking and Loan. The only other bank in a two-county radius had mysteriously burned down, and with the onset of the Depression, it never reopened. Though everyone knew what had really happened, not a word was ever spoken for fear of retribution, and their fear was well placed. The bank wasn't the only building that had mysteriously burned down.

His interest rates were outrageous, and little by little he began amassing more land and property as people defaulted on their loans. When the Depression hit hardest, he foreclosed on dozens of businesses throughout the county while retaining the original owners to continue to work on salary, paying them just enough to keep them where they were, because they had nowhere else to go. He told them that when the economy improved, he'd sell their business back to them, and people always believed him.

Never once, however, did he keep his promise. In the end he controlled a vast portion of the county's economy, and he abused his clout in every way imaginable.

I'd like to tell you he eventually went to a terrible

death, but he didn't. He died at a ripe-old age while
sleeping with his mistress on his yacht off the Cayman
Islands. He'd outlived both his wives and his only son.
Some end for a guy like that, huh? Life, I've learned,
is never fair. If people teach anything in school, that
should be it.

But back to the story.... Hegbert, once he realized
what a bastard my grandfather really was, quit working for him and went into the ministry, then came
back to Beaufort and started ministering in the same
church we attended. He spent his first few years per-
fecting his fire-and-brimstone act with monthly sermons on the evils of the greedy, and this left him scant
time for anything else. He was forty-three before he
ever got married; he was fifty-five when his daughter,
Jamie Sullivan, was born. His wife, a wispy little thing
twenty years younger than he, went through six miscarriages before Jamie was born, and in the end she
died in childbirth, making Hegbert a widower who had
to raise a daughter on his own.

Hence, of course, the story behind the play.

People knew the story even before the play was
first performed. It was one of those stories that made
its rounds whenever Hegbert had to baptize a baby or
attend a funeral. Everyone knew about it, and that's
why, I think, so many people got emotional whenever
they saw the Christmas play. They knew it was based
on something that happened in real life, which gave it
special meaning.

Jamie Sullivan was a senior in high school, just like
me, and she'd already been chosen to play the angel,
not that anyone else even had a chance. This, of course,

made the play extra special that year. It was going to be a big deal, maybe the biggest ever—at least in Miss Garber's mind. She was the drama teacher, and she was already glowing about the possibilities the first time I met her in class.

Now, I hadn't really planned on taking drama that year. I really hadn't, but it was either that or chemistry II. The thing was, I thought it would be a blow-off class, especially when compared with my other option. No papers, no tests, no tables where I'd have to memorize protons and neutrons and combine elements in their proper formulas . . . what could possibly be better for a high school senior? It seemed like a sure thing, and when I signed up for it, I thought I'd just be able to sleep through most every class, which, considering my late night peanut eating, was fairly important at the time.

On the first day of class I was one of the last to arrive, coming in just a few seconds before the bell rang, and I took a seat in the back of the room. Miss Garber had her back turned to the class, and she was busy writing her name in big cursive letters, as if we didn't know who she was. Everyone knew her—it was impossible not to. She was big, at least six feet two, with flaming red hair and pale skin that showed her freckles well into her forties. She was also overweight—I'd say honestly she pushed two fifty—and she had a fondness for wearing flower-patterned muumuus. She had thick, dark, horn-rimmed glasses, and she greeted every one with, "Helloooooo," sort of singing the last syllable. Miss Garber was one of a kind, that's for sure, and she was single, which made it even worse. A guy, no matter how old, couldn't help but feel sorry for a gal like her.

Beneath her name she wrote the goals she wanted to accomplish that year. "Self-confidence" was number one, followed by "Self-awareness" and, third, "Self-fulfillment." Miss Garber was big into the "self" stuff, which put her really ahead of the curve as far as psychotherapy is concerned, though she probably didn't realize it at the time. Miss Garber was a pioneer in that field. Maybe it had something to do with the way she looked; maybe she was just trying to feel better about herself.

But I digress.

It wasn't until the class started that I noticed something unusual. Though Beaufort High School wasn't large, I knew for a fact that it was pretty much split fifty-fifty between males and females, which was why I was surprised when I saw that this class was at least ninety percent female. There was only one other male in the class, which to my thinking was a good thing, and for a moment I felt flush with a "look out world, here I come" kind of feeling. Girls, girls, girls...I couldn't help but think. Girls and girls and no tests in sight.

Okay, so I wasn't the most forward-thinking guy on the block.

So Miss Garber brings up the Christmas play and tells everyone that Jamie Sullivan is going to be the angel that year. Miss Garber started clapping right away—she was a member of the church, too—and there were a lot of people who thought she was gunning for Hegbert in a romantic sort of way. The first time I heard it, I remember thinking that it was a good thing they were too old to have children, if they ever did get together. Imagine—translucent with freckles? The very thought gave everyone shudders, but of course, no one ever said anything about it, at least within hearing distance of Miss Garber and Hegbert. Gossip is one thing, hurtful gossip is completely another, and even in high school we weren't *that* mean.

Miss Garber kept on clapping, all alone for a while, until all of us finally joined in, because it was obvious that was what she wanted. "Stand up, Jamie," she said. So Jamie stood up and turned around, and Miss Garber started clapping even faster, as if she were standing in the presence of a bona fide movie star.

Now Jamie Sullivan was a nice girl. She really was. Beaufort was small enough that it had only one elementary school, so we'd been in the same classes our entire lives, and I'd be lying if I said I never talked to her. Once, in second grade, she'd sat in the seat right next to me for the whole year, and we'd even had a few conversations, but it didn't mean that I spent a lot of time hanging out with her in my spare time, even back then. Who I saw in school was one thing; who I saw *after* school was something completely different, and Jamie had never been on my social calendar.

It's not that Jamie was unattractive—don't get me wrong. She wasn't hideous or anything like that. Fortunately she'd taken after her mother, who, based on the pictures I'd seen, wasn't half-bad, especially considering who she ended up marrying. But Jamie wasn't exactly what I considered attractive, either. Despite the fact that she was thin, with honey blond hair and soft blue eyes, most of the time she looked sort of . . . *plain*, and that was when you noticed her at all. Jamie didn't care much about outward appearances, because she was always looking for things like "inner beauty," and I suppose that's part of the reason she looked the way she did. For as long as I'd known her—and this was going way back, remember—she'd always worn her hair in a tight bun, almost like a spinster, without a stitch of makeup on her face. Coupled with her usual brown cardigan and plaid skirt, she always looked as though she were on her way to interview for a job at the library. We used to think it was just a phase and that she'd eventually grow out of it, but she never had. Even through our first three years of high school, she hadn't changed at all. The only thing that had changed was the size of her clothes.

But it wasn't just the way Jamie looked that made her different; it was also the way she acted. Jamie didn't spend any time hanging out at Cecil's Diner or going to slumber parties with other girls, and I knew for a fact that she'd never had a boyfriend her entire life. Old Hegbert would probably have had a heart attack if she had. But even if by some odd turn of events Hegbert had allowed it, it still wouldn't have mattered. Jamie carried her Bible wherever she went, and if her looks and Hegbert didn't keep the boys away, the Bible sure as heck did. Now, I liked the Bible as much as the next teenage boy, but Jamie seemed to enjoy it in a way that was completely foreign to me. Not only did she go to vacation Bible school every August, but she would read the Bible during lunch break at school. In my mind that just wasn't normal, even if she was the minister's daughter. No matter how you sliced it, reading Paul's letters to the Ephesians wasn't nearly as much fun as flirting, if you know what I mean.

But Jamie didn't stop there. Because of all her Bible reading, or maybe because of Hegbert's influence, Jamie believed it was important to help others, and helping others is exactly what she did. I knew she volunteered at the orphanage in Morehead City, but for her that simply wasn't enough. She was always in charge of one fund-raiser or another, helping everyone from the Boy Scouts to the Indian Princesses, and I know that when she was fourteen, she spent part of her summer painting the outside of an elderly neighbor's house. Jamie was the kind of girl who would pull weeds in someone's garden without being asked or stop traffic to help little kids cross the road. She'd save her allowance to buy a new basketball for the orphans, or she'd turn around and drop the money into the church basket on Sunday. She was, in other words, the kind of girl who made the rest of us look bad, and whenever she glanced my way, I couldn't help but feel guilty, even though I hadn't done anything wrong.

Nor did Jamie limit her good deeds to people. If she ever came across a wounded animal, for instance, she'd try to help it, too. Opossums, squirrels, dogs, cats, frogs ... it didn't matter to her. Dr. Rawlings, the vet, knew her by sight, and he'd shake his head whenever he saw her walking up to the door carrying a cardboard box with yet another critter inside. He'd take off his eyeglasses and wipe them with his handkerchief while Jamie explained how she'd found the poor creature and what had happened to it. "He was hit by a car, Dr. Rawlings. I think it was in the Lord's plan to have me find him and try to save him. You'll help me, won't you?"

With Jamie, everything was in the Lord's plan. That was another thing. She always mentioned the Lord's plan whenever you talked to her, no matter what the subject. The baseball game's rained out? Must be the Lord's plan to prevent something worse from happening. A surprise trigonometry quiz that everyone in class fails? Must be in the Lord's plan to give us challenges. Anyway, you get the picture.

Then, of course, there was the whole Hegbert situation, and this didn't help her at all. Being the minister's daughter couldn't have been easy, but she made it seem as if it were the most natural thing in the world and that she was lucky to have been blessed in that way. That's how she used to say it, too. "I've been so blessed to have a father like mine." Whenever she said it, all we could do was shake our heads and wonder what planet she actually came from.

Despite all these other strikes, though, the one thing that *really* drove me crazy about her was the fact that she was always so damn cheerful, no matter what was happening around her. I swear, that girl never said a bad thing about anything or anyone, even to those of us who weren't that nice to her. She would hum to herself as she walked down the street, she would wave to strangers driving by in their cars. Sometimes ladies would come running out of their house if they saw her walking by, offering her pumpkin bread if they'd been baking all day or lemonade if the sun was high in the sky. It seemed as if every adult in town adored her. "She's such a nice young lady," they'd say whenever Jamie's name came up. "The world would be a better place if there were more people like her."

But my friends and I didn't quite see it that way. In our minds, one Jamie Sullivan was plenty.

I was thinking about all this while Jamie stood in front of us on the first day of drama class, and I admit that I wasn't much interested in seeing her. But strangely, when Jamie turned to face us, I kind of got a shock, like I was sitting on a loose wire or something. She wore a plaid skirt with a white blouse under the same brown cardigan sweater I'd seen a million times, but there were two new bumps on her chest that the sweater couldn't hide that I swore hadn't been there just three months earlier. She'd never worn makeup and she still didn't, but she had a tan, probably from Bible school, and for the first time she looked—well, almost pretty. Of course, I dismissed that thought right away, but as she looked around the room, she stopped and smiled right at me, obviously glad to see that I was in the class. It wasn't until later that I would learn the reason why.

Two

After high school I planned to go to the University of North Carolina at Chapel Hill. My father wanted me to go to Harvard or Princeton like some of the sons of other congressmen did, but with my grades it wasn't possible. Not that I was a bad student. I just didn't focus on my studies, and my grades weren't exactly up to snuff for the Ivy Leagues. By my senior year it was pretty much touch and go whether I'd even get accepted at UNC, and this was my father's alma mater, a place where he could pull some strings. During one of his few weekends home, my father came up with the plan to put me over the top. I'd just finished my first week of school and we were sitting down for dinner. He was home for three days on account of Labor Day weekend.

"I think you should run for student body president," he said. "You'll be graduating in June, and I think it would look good on your record. Your mother thinks so, too, by the way."

My mother nodded as she chewed a mouthful of peas. She didn't speak much when my father had the floor, though she winked at me. Sometimes I think my mother liked to see me squirm, even though she was sweet.

"I don't think I'd have a chance at winning," I said. Though I was probably the richest kid in school, I was by no means the most popular. That honor belonged to Eric Hunter, my best friend. He could throw a baseball at almost ninety miles an hour, and he'd led the football team to back-to-back state titles as the star quarterback. He was a stud. Even his name sounded cool.

"Of course you can win," my father said quickly. "We Carters always win."

That's another one of the reasons I didn't like spending time with my father. During those few times he was home, I think he wanted to mold me into a miniature version of himself. Since I'd grown up pretty much without him, I'd come to resent having him around. This was the first conversation we'd had in weeks. He rarely talked to me on the phone.

"But what if I don't want to?"

My father put down his fork, a bite of his pork chop still on the tines. He looked at me crossly, giving me the once-over. He was wearing a suit even though it was over eighty degrees in the house, and it made him even more intimidating. My father always wore a suit, by the way.

"I think," he said slowly, "that it would be a good idea."

I knew that when he talked that way the issue was settled. That's the way it was in my family. My father's word was law. But the fact was, even after I agreed, I didn't want to do it. I didn't want to waste my afternoons meeting with teachers after school—after school!—every week for the rest of the year, dreaming up themes for school dances or trying to decide what colors the streamers should be. That's really all the class presidents did, at least back when I was in high school. It wasn't like students had the power to actually decide anything meaningful.

But then again, I knew my father had a point. If I wanted to go to UNC, I had to do something. I didn't play football or basketball, I didn't play an instrument, I wasn't in the chess club or the bowling club or anything else. I didn't excel in the classroom—hell, I didn't excel at much of anything. Growing despondent, I started listing the things I actually could do, but to be honest, there really wasn't that much. I could tie eight different types of sailing knots, I could walk barefoot across hot asphalt farther than anyone I knew, I could balance a pencil vertically on my finger for thirty seconds...but I didn't think that any of those things would really stand out on a college application. So there I was, lying in bed all night long, slowly coming to the sinking realization that I was a loser. Thanks, Dad.

The next morning I went to the principal's office and added my name to the list of candidates. There were two other people running—John Foreman and Maggie Brown. Now, John didn't stand a chance, I knew that right off. He was the kind of guy who'd pick lint off your clothes while he talked to you. But he was a good student. He sat in the front row and raised his hand every time the teacher asked a question. If he was called to give the answer, he would almost always give the right one, and he'd turn his head from side to side with a smug look on his face, as if proving how superior his intellect was when compared with those of the other peons in the room. Eric and I used to shoot spitballs at him when the teacher's back was turned.

Maggie Brown was another matter. She was a good student as well. She'd served on the student council for the first three years and had been the junior class president the year before. The only real strike against her was the fact that she wasn't very attractive, and she'd put on twenty pounds that summer. I knew that not a single guy would vote for her.

After seeing the competition, I figured that I might have a chance after all. My entire future was on the line here, so I formulated my strategy. Eric was the first to agree.

"Sure, I'll get all the guys on the team to vote for you, no problem. If that's what you really want."

"How about their girlfriends, too?" I asked.

That was pretty much my entire campaign. Of course, I went to the debates like I was supposed to, and I passed out those dorky "What I'll do if I'm elected president" fliers, but in the end it was Eric Hunter who probably got me where I needed to be. Beaufort High School had only about four hundred students, so getting the athletic vote was critical, and most of the jocks didn't give a hoot who they voted for anyway. In the end it worked out just the way I planned.

I was voted student body president with a fairly large majority of the vote. I had no idea what trouble it would eventually lead me to.

*   *   *

When I was a junior I went steady with a girl named Angela Clark. She was my first real girlfriend, though it lasted for only a few months. Just before school let out for the summer, she dumped me for a guy named Lew who was twenty years old and worked as a mechanic in his father's garage. His primary attribute, as far as I could tell, was that he had a really nice car. He always wore a white T-shirt with a pack of Camels folded into the sleeve, and he'd lean against the hood of his Thunderbird, looking back and forth, saying things like "Hey, baby" whenever a girl walked by. He was a real winner, if you know what I mean.

Well, anyway, the homecoming dance was coming up, and because of the whole Angela situation, I still didn't have a date. Everyone on the student council had to attend—it was mandatory. I had to help decorate the gym and clean up the next day—and besides, it was usually a pretty good time. I called a couple of girls I knew, but they already had dates, so I called a few more. They had dates, too. By the final week the pickings were getting pretty slim. The pool was down to the kinds of girls who had thick glasses and talked with lisps. Beaufort was never exactly a hotbed for beauties anyway, but then again I had to find somebody. I didn't want to go to the dance without a date—what would that look like? I'd be the only student body president ever to attend the homecoming dance alone. I'd end up being the guy scooping punch all night long or mopping up the barf in the bathroom. That's what people without dates usually did.

Growing sort of panicky, I pulled out the yearbook

from the year before and started flipping through the pages one by one, looking for anyone who might not have a date. First I looked through the pages with the seniors. Though a lot of them were off at college, a few of them were still around town. Even though I didn't think I had much of a chance with them, I called anyway, and sure enough, I was proven right. I couldn't find anyone, at least not anyone who would go with me. I was getting pretty good at handling rejection, I'll tell you, though that's not the sort of thing you brag about to your grandkids. My mom knew what I was going through, and she finally came into my room and sat on the bed beside me.

"If you can't get a date, I'll be happy to go with you," she said.

"Thanks, Mom," I said dejectedly.

When she left the room, I felt even worse than I had before. Even my mom didn't think I could find somebody. And if I showed up with her? If I lived a hundred years, I'd never live that down.

There was another guy in my boat, by the way. Carey Dennison had been elected treasurer, and he still didn't have a date, either. Carey was the kind of guy no one wanted to spend time with at all, and the only reason he'd been elected was because he'd run unopposed. Even then I think the vote was fairly close. He played the tuba in the marching band, and his body looked all out of proportion, as if he'd stopped growing halfway through puberty. He had a great big stomach and gangly arms and legs, like the Hoos in Hooville, if you know what I mean. He also had a high-pitched way of talking—it's what made him such a good tuba player, I reckon—and he never stopped asking questions. "Where did you go last weekend? Was it fun? Did you see any girls?" He wouldn't even wait for an answer, and he'd move around constantly as he asked so you had to keep turning your head to keep him in sight. I swear he was probably the most annoying person I'd ever met. If I didn't get a date, he'd stand off on one side with me all night long, firing questions like some deranged prosecutor.

So there I was, flipping through the pages in the junior class section, when I saw Jamie Sullivan's picture. I paused for just a second, then turned the page, cursing myself for even thinking about it. I spent the next hour searching for anyone halfway decent looking, but I slowly came to the realization that there wasn't anyone left. In time I finally turned back to her picture and looked again. She wasn't bad looking, I told myself, and she's really sweet. She'd probably say yes, I thought. . . .

I closed the yearbook. Jamie Sullivan? Hegbert's daughter? No way. Absolutely not. My friends would roast me alive.

But compared with dating your mother or cleaning up puke or even, God forbid . . . Carey Dennison?

I spent the rest of the evening debating the pros and cons of my dilemma. Believe me, I went back and forth for a while, but in the end the choice was obvious, even to me. I had to ask Jamie to the dance, and I paced around the room thinking of the best way to ask her.

It was then that I realized something terrible, something absolutely frightening. Carey Dennison, I suddenly realized, was probably doing the exact same thing I was doing right now. He was probably looking through the yearbook, too! He was weird, but he wasn't the kind of guy who liked cleaning up puke, either, and if you'd seen his mother, you'd know that his choice was even worse than mine. What if he asked Jamie first? Jamie wouldn't say no to him, and realistically she was the only option he had. No one besides her would be caught dead with him. Jamie helped everyone—she was one of those equal opportunity saints. She'd probably listen to Carey's squeaky voice, see the goodness radiating from his heart, and accept right off the bat.

So there I was, sitting in my room, frantic with the possibility that Jamie might not go to the dance with me. I barely slept that night, I tell you, which was just about the strangest thing I'd ever experienced. I don't think anyone ever fretted about asking Jamie out before. I planned to ask her first thing in the morning, while I still had my courage, but Jamie wasn't in school. I assumed she was working with the orphans over in Morehead City, the way she did every month. A few of us had tried to get out of school using that excuse, too, but Jamie was the only one who ever got away with it. The principal knew she was reading to them or doing crafts or just sitting around playing games with them. She wasn't sneaking out to the beach or hanging out at Cecil's Diner or anything. That concept was absolutely ludicrous.

"Got a date yet?" Eric asked me in between classes. He knew very well that I didn't, but even though he was my best friend, he liked to stick it to me once in a while.

"Not yet," I said, "but I'm working on it."

Down the hall, Carey Dennison was reaching into his locker. I swear he shot me a beady glare when he thought I wasn't looking.

That's the kind of day it was.

The minutes ticked by slowly during my final class. The way I figured it—if Carey and I got out at the same time, I'd be able to get to her house first, what with those gawky legs and all. I started to psych myself up, and when the bell rang, I took off from school running at a full clip. I was flying for about a hundred yards or so, and then I started to get kind of tired, and then a cramp set in. Pretty soon all I could do was walk, but that cramp really started to get to me, and I had to bend over and hold my side while I kept moving. As I made my way down the streets of Beaufort, I looked like a wheezing version of the Hunchback of Notre Dame.

Behind me I thought I heard Carey's high-pitched laughter. I turned around, digging my fingers into my gut to stifle the pain, but I couldn't see him. Maybe he was cutting through someone's backyard! He was a sneaky bastard, that guy. You couldn't trust him even for a minute.

I started to stumble along even faster, and pretty soon I reached Jamie's street. By then I was sweating all over—my shirt was soaked right through—and I was still wheezing something fierce. Well, I reached her front door, took a second to catch my breath, and finally knocked. Despite my fevered rush to her house, my pessimistic side assumed that Carey would be the one who opened the door for me. I imagined him smiling at me with a victorious look in his eye, one that essentially meant "Sorry, partner, you're too late."

But it wasn't Carey who answered, it was Jamie, and for the first time in my life I saw what she'd look like if she were an ordinary person. She was wearing jeans and a red blouse, and though her hair was still pulled up into a bun, she looked more casual than she usually did. I realized she could actually be cute if she gave herself the opportunity.

"Landon," she said as she held open the door, "this is a surprise!" Jamie was always glad to see everyone, including me, though I think my appearance startled her. "You look like you've been exercising," she said.

"Not really," I lied, wiping my brow. Luckily the cramp was fading fast.

"You've sweat clean through your shirt."

"Oh, that?" I looked at my shirt. "That's nothing. I just sweat a lot sometimes."

"Maybe you should have it checked by a doctor."

"I'll be okay, I'm sure."

"I'll say a prayer for you anyway," she offered as she smiled. Jamie was always praying for someone. I might as well join the club.

"Thanks," I said.

She looked down and sort of shuffled her feet for a moment. "Well, I'd invite you in, but my father isn't home, and he doesn't allow boys in the house while he's not around."

"Oh," I said dejectedly, "that's okay. We can talk out here, I guess." If I'd had my way, I would have done this inside.

"Would you like some lemonade while we sit?" she asked. "I just made some."

"I'd love some," I said.

"I'll be right back." She walked back into the house, but she left the door open and I took a quick glance around. The house, I noticed, was small but tidy, with a piano against one wall and a sofa against the other. A small fan sat oscillating in the corner. On the coffee table there were books with names like *Listening to Jesus* and *Faith Is the Answer.* Her Bible was there, too, and it was opened to the chapter on Luke.

A moment later Jamie returned with the lemonade, and we took a seat in two chairs near the corner of the porch. I knew she and her father sat there in the evenings because I passed by their house now and then. As soon as we were seated, I saw Mrs. Hastings, her neighbor across the street, wave to us. Jamie waved back while I sort of scooted my chair so that Mrs. Hastings couldn't see my face. Even though I was going to ask Jamie to the dance, I didn't want anyone—even Mrs. Hastings—to see me there on the off chance that she'd already accepted Carey's offer. It was one thing to actually go with Jamie, it was another thing to be rejected by her in favor of a guy like Carey.

"What are you doing?" Jamie asked me. "You're moving your chair into the sun."

"I like the sun," I said. She was right, though. Almost immediately I could feel the rays burning through my shirt and making me sweat again.

"If that's what you want," she said, smiling. "So, what did you want to talk to me about?"

Jamie reached up and started to adjust her hair. By my reckoning, it hadn't moved at all. I took a deep breath, trying to gather myself, but I couldn't force myself to come out with it just yet.

"So," I said instead, "you were at the orphanage today?"

Jamie looked at me curiously. "No. My father and I were at the doctor's office."

"Is he okay?"

She smiled. "Healthy as can be."

I nodded and glanced across the street. Mrs. Hastings had gone back inside, and I couldn't see anyone else in the vicinity. The coast was finally clear, but I still wasn't ready.

"Sure is a beautiful day," I said, stalling.

"Yes, it is."

"Warm, too."

"That's because you're in the sun."

I looked around, feeling the pressure building. "Why, I'll bet there's not a single cloud in the whole sky."

This time Jamie didn't respond, and we sat in silence for a few moments.

"Landon," she finally said, "you didn't come here to talk about the weather, did you?"

"Not really."

"Then why are you here?"

The moment of truth had arrived, and I cleared my throat.

"Well... I wanted to know if you were going to the homecoming dance."

"Oh," she said. Her tone made it seem as if she were unaware that such a thing existed. I fidgeted in my seat and waited for her answer.

"I really hadn't planned on going," she finally said.

"But if someone asked you to go, you might?"

It took a moment for her to answer.

"I'm not sure," she said, thinking carefully. "I suppose I might go, if I got the chance. I've never been to a home-coming dance before."

"They're fun," I said quickly. "Not *too* much fun, but fun." Especially when compared to my other options, I didn't add.

She smiled at my turn of phrase. "I'd have to talk to my father, of course, but if he said it was okay, then I guess I could."

In the tree beside the porch, a bird started to chirp noisily, as if he knew I wasn't supposed to be here. I concentrated on the sound, trying to calm my nerves. Just two days ago I couldn't have imagined myself even thinking about it, but suddenly there I was, listening to myself as I spoke the magic words.

"Well, would you like to go to the dance with me?"

I could tell she was surprised. I think she believed that the little lead-up to the question probably had to do with someone else asking her. Sometimes teenagers sent their friends out to "scout the terrain," so to speak, so as not to face possible rejection. Even though Jamie wasn't much like other teenagers, I'm sure she was familiar with the concept, at least in theory.

Instead of answering right away, though, Jamie glanced away for a long moment. I got a sinking feeling in my stomach because I assumed she was going to say no. Visions of my mother, puke, and Carey flooded through my mind, and all of a sudden I regretted the way I'd behaved toward her all these years. I kept remembering all the times I'd teased her or called her father a fornicator or simply made fun of her behind her back. Just when I was feeling awful about the whole thing and imagining how I would ever be able to avoid Carey for five hours, she turned and faced me again. She had a slight smile on her face.

"I'd love to," she finally said, "on one condition."

I steadied myself, hoping it wasn't something *too* awful.

"Yes?"

"You have to promise that you won't fall in love with me."

I knew she was kidding by the way she laughed, and I couldn't help but breathe a sigh of relief. Sometimes, I had to admit, Jamie had a pretty good sense of humor.

I smiled and gave her my word.

Three

As a general rule, Southern Baptists don't dance. In Beaufort, however, it wasn't a rule that was ever strictly enforced. The minister before Hegbert—don't ask me what his name was—took sort of a lax view about school dances as long as they were chaperoned, and because of that, they'd become a tradition of sorts. By the time Hegbert came along, it was too late to change things. Jamie was pretty much the only one who'd never been to a school dance and frankly, I didn't know whether she even knew how to dance at all.

I admit that I also had some concerns about what she would wear, though it wasn't something I would tell her. When Jamie went to the church socials—which were encouraged by Hegbert—she usually wore an old sweater and one of the plaid skirts we saw in school every day, but the homecoming dance was supposed to be special. Most of the girls bought new dresses and the boys wore suits, and this year we were bringing in a photographer to take our pictures. I knew Jamie wasn't going to buy a new dress because she wasn't exactly well-off. Ministering wasn't a profession where people made a lot of money, but of course ministers weren't in it for monetary gain, they were in it for the long haul, if you know what I mean. But I didn't want her to wear the same thing she wore to school every day, either. Not so much for me—I'm not that cold-hearted—but because of what others might say. I didn't want people to make fun of her or anything.

The good news, if there was any, was that Eric didn't rib me too bad about the whole Jamie situation because he was too busy thinking about his own date. He was taking Margaret Hays, who was the head cheerleader at our school. She wasn't the brightest bulb on the Christmas tree, but she was nice in her own way. By nice, of course, I'm talking about her legs. Eric offered to double-date with me, but I turned him down because I didn't want to take any chances with Eric teasing Jamie or anything like that. He was a good guy, but he could be kind of heartless sometimes, especially when he had a few shots of bourbon in him.

The day of the dance was actually quite busy for me. I spent most of the afternoon helping to decorate the gym, and I had to get to Jamie's about a half hour early because her father wanted to talk to me, though I didn't know why. Jamie had sprung that one on me just the day before, and I can't say I was exactly thrilled by the prospect of it. I figured he was going to talk about temptation and the evil path it can lead us to. If he brought up fornication, though, I knew I would die right there on the spot. I said small prayers all day long in the hope of avoiding this conversation, but I wasn't sure if God would put my prayers on the front burner, if you know what I mean, because of the way I'd behaved in the past. I was pretty nervous just thinking about it.

After I showered I put on my best suit, swung by the florist to pick up Jamie's corsage, then drove to her house. My mom had let me borrow the car, and I parked it on the street directly in front of Jamie's house. We hadn't turned the clocks back yet, so it was still light out when I got there, and I strolled up the cracked walkway to her door. I knocked and waited for a moment, then knocked again. From behind the door I heard Hegbert say, "I'll be right there," but he wasn't exactly racing to the door. I must have stood there for two minutes or so, looking at the door, the moldings, the little cracks in the windowsills. Off to the side were the chairs that Jamie and I had sat in just a few days back. The one I sat in was still turned in the opposite direction. I guess they hadn't sat there in the last couple of days.

Finally the door creaked open. The light coming from the lamp inside shadowed Hegbert's face slightly and sort of reflected through his hair. He was old, like I said, seventy-two years by my reckoning. It was the first time I'd ever seen him up close, and I could see all the wrinkles on his face. His skin really was translucent, even more so than I'd imagined.

"Hello, Reverend," I said, swallowing my trepidation. "I'm here to take Jamie to the homecoming dance."

"Of course you are," he said. "But first, I wanted to talk with you."

"Yes, sir, that's why I came early."

"C'mon in."

In church Hegbert was a fairly snappy dresser, but right now he looked like a farmer, dressed in overalls and a T-shirt. He motioned for me to sit on the wooden chair he'd brought in from the kitchen. "I'm sorry it took a little while to open the door. I was working on tomorrow's sermon," he said.

I sat down.

"That's okay, sir." I don't know why, but you just had to call him "sir." He sort of projected that image.

"All right, then, so tell me about yourself."

I thought it was a fairly ridiculous question, with him having such a long history with my family and all. He was also the one who had baptized me, by the way, and he'd seen me in church every Sunday since I'd been a baby.

"Well, sir," I began, not really knowing what to say, "I'm the student body president. I don't know whether Jamie mentioned that to you."

He nodded. "She did. Go on."

"And ... well, I hope to go to the University of North Carolina next fall. I've already received the application."

He nodded again. "Anything else?"

I had to admit, I was running out of things after that. Part of me wanted to pick up the pencil off the end table and start balancing it, giving him the whole thirty seconds' worth, but he wasn't the kind of guy who would appreciate it.

"I guess not, sir."

"Do you mind if I ask you a question?"

"No, sir."

He sort of stared at me for a long time, as if thinking about it.

"Why did you ask my daughter to the dance?" he finally said.

I was surprised, and I know that my expression showed it.

"I don't know what you mean, sir."

"You're not planning to do anything to...embarrass her, are you?"

"No, sir," I said quickly, shocked by the accusation. "Not at all. I needed someone to go with, and I asked her. It's as simple as that."

"You don't have any pranks planned?"

"No, sir. I wouldn't do that to her..."

This went on for a few more minutes—his grilling me about my true intentions, I mean—but luckily Jamie stepped out of the back room, and her father and I both turned our heads at the same moment. Hegbert finally stopped talking, and I breathed a sigh of relief. She'd put on a nice blue skirt and a white blouse I'd never seen before. Fortunately she'd left her sweater in the closet. It wasn't too bad, I had to admit, though I knew she'd still be underdressed compared with others at the dance. As always, her hair was pulled up in a bun. Personally I think it would have looked better if she'd kept it down, but that was the last thing I wanted to say. Jamie looked like...well, Jamie looked exactly like she usually did, but at least she wasn't planning on bringing her Bible. That would have just been too much to live down.

"You're not giving Landon a hard time, are you?" she said cheerfully to her father.

"We were just visiting," I said quickly before he had a chance to respond. For some reason I didn't think he'd told Jamie about the kind of person he thought I was, and I didn't think that now would be a good time.

"Well, we should probably go," she said after a moment. I think she sensed the tension in the room. She walked over to her father and kissed him on the cheek. "Don't stay up too late working on the sermon, okay?"

"I won't," he said softly. Even with me in the room, I could tell he really loved her and wasn't afraid to show it. It was how he felt about me that was the problem.

We said good-bye, and on our way to the car I handed Jamie her corsage and told her I'd show her how to put it on once we got in the car. I opened her door for her and walked around the other side, then got in as well. In that short period of time, Jamie had already pinned on the flower.

"I'm not exactly a dimwit, you know. I do know how to pin on a corsage."

I started the car and headed toward the high school, with the conversation I'd just had with Hegbert running through my mind.

"My father doesn't like you very much," she said, as if knowing what I was thinking.

I nodded without saying anything.

"He thinks you're irresponsible."

I nodded again.

"He doesn't like your father much, either."

I nodded once more.

"Or your family."

I get the picture.

"But do you know what I think?" she asked suddenly.

"Not really." By then I was pretty depressed.

"I think that all this was in the Lord's plan somehow. What do you think the message is?"

Here we go, I thought to myself.

I doubt if the evening could have been much worse, if
you want to know the truth. Most of my friends kept
their distance, and Jamie didn't have many friends to
begin with, so we spent most of our time alone. Even
worse, it turned out that my presence wasn't even
required anymore. They'd changed the rule owing to
the fact that Carey couldn't get a date, and that left
me feeling pretty miserable about the whole thing as
soon as I found out about it. But because of what her
father had said to me, I couldn't exactly take her home
early, now, could I? And more than that, she was really
having a good time; even I could see that. She loved
the decorations I'd helped put up, she loved the music,
she loved everything about the dance. She kept telling
me how wonderful everything was, and she asked me
whether I might help her decorate the church someday, for one of their socials. I sort of mumbled that
she should call me, and even though I said it without a
trace of energy, Jamie thanked me for being so consid-
erate. To be honest, I was depressed for at least the first
hour, though she didn't seem to notice.

Jamie had to be home by eleven o'clock, an hour
before the dance ended, which made it somewhat easier for me to handle. Once the music started we hit
the floor, and it turned out that she was a pretty good
dancer, considering it was her first time and all. She
followed my lead pretty well through about a dozen
songs, and after that we headed to the tables and had

what resembled an ordinary conversation. Sure, she threw in words like "faith" and "joy" and even "salvation," and she talked about helping the orphans and scooping critters off the highway, but she was just so damn happy, it was hard to stay down for long.

So things weren't too terrible at first and really no worse than I had expected. It wasn't until Lew and Angela showed up that everything really went sour.

They showed up a few minutes after we arrived. He was wearing that stupid T-shirt, Camels in his sleeve, and a glop of hair gel on his head. Angela hung all over him right from the beginning of the dance, and it didn't take a genius to realize she'd had a few drinks before she got there. Her dress was really flashy—her mother worked in a salon and was up on all the latest fashions—and I noticed she'd picked up that ladylike habit called chewing gum. She really worked that gum, chewing it almost like a cow working her cud.

Well, good old Lew spiked the punch bowl, and a few more people started getting tipsy. By the time the teachers found out, most of the punch was already gone and people were getting that glassy look in their eyes. When I saw Angela gobble up her second glass of punch, I knew I should keep my eye on her. Even though she'd dumped me, I didn't want anything bad to happen to her. She was the first girl I'd ever French-kissed, and even though our teeth clanked together so hard the first time we tried it that I saw stars and had to take aspirin when I got home, I still had feelings for her.

So there I was, sitting with Jamie, barely listening as she described the wonders of Bible school, watching Angela out of the corner of my eye, when Lew spotted me looking at her. In one frenzied motion he grabbed Angela around the waist and dragged her over to the table, giving me one of those looks, the one that "means business." You know the one I'm talking about.

"Are you staring at my girl?" he asked, already tensing up.

"No."

"Yeah, he was," Angela said, kind of slurring out the words. "He was staring right at me. This is my old boyfriend, the one I told you about."

His eyes turned into little slits, just like Hegbert's were prone to do. I guess I have this effect on lots of people.

"So you're the one," he said, sneering.

Now, I'm not much of a fighter. The only real fight I was ever in was in third grade, and I pretty much lost that one when I started to cry even before the guy punched me. Usually I didn't have much trouble staying away from things like this because of my passive nature, and besides, no one ever messed with me when Eric was around. But Eric was off with Margaret somewhere, probably behind the bleachers.

"I wasn't staring," I said finally, "and I don't know what she told you, but I doubt if it was true."

His eyes narrowed. "Are you calling Angela a liar?" he sneered.

Oops.

I think he would have hit me right there, but Jamie suddenly worked her way into the situation.

"Don't I know you?" she said cheerfully, looking right at him. Sometimes Jamie seemed oblivious of situations that were happening right in front of her.

"Wait—yes, I do. You work in the garage downtown. Your father's name is Joe, and your grandma lives out on Foster Road, by the railroad crossing."

A look of confusion crossed Lew's face, as though he were trying to put together a puzzle with too many pieces.

"How do you know all that? What he'd do, tell you about me, too?"

"No," Jamie said, "don't be silly." She laughed to herself. Only Jamie could find humor at a time like this. "I saw your picture in your grandma's house. I was walking by, and she needed some help bringing in the groceries. Your picture was on the mantel."

Lew was looking at Jamie as though she had cornstalks growing out of her ears.

Meanwhile Jamie was fanning herself with her hand. "Well, we were just sitting down to take a breather from all that dancing. It sure gets hot out there. Would you like to join us? We've got a couple of chairs. I'd love to hear how your grandma is doing."

She sounded so happy about it that Lew didn't know what to do. Unlike those of us who were used to this sort of thing, he'd never come across someone like Jamie before. He stood there for a moment or two, trying to decide if he should hit the guy with the girl who'd helped his grandma. If it sounds confusing to you, imagine what it was doing to Lew's petroleum-damaged brain.

He finally skulked off without responding, taking Angela with him. Angela had probably forgotten how the whole thing started anyway, owing to the amount she'd had to drink. Jamie and I watched him go, and when he was a safe distance away, I exhaled. I hadn't even realized I'd been holding my breath.

"Thanks," I mumbled sheepishly, realizing that Jamie—Jamie!—was the one who'd saved me from grave bodily harm.

Jamie looked at me strangely. "For what?" she asked, and when I didn't exactly spell it out for her, she went right back into her story about Bible school, as if nothing had happened at all. But this time I found myself actually listening to her, at least with one of my ears. It was the least I could do.

It turns out that it wasn't the last we saw of either Lew or Angela that evening. The two glasses of punch had really done Angela in, and she threw up all over the ladies' rest room. Lew, being the classy guy he was, left when he heard her retching, sort of slinking out the way he came in, and that was the last I saw of him. Jamie, as fate would have it, was the one who found Angela in the bathroom, and it was obvious that Angela wasn't doing too well. The only option was to clean her up and take her home before the teachers found out about it. Getting drunk was a big deal back then, and she'd be looking at suspension, maybe even expulsion, if she got caught.

Jamie, bless her heart, didn't want that to happen any more than I did, though I would have thought otherwise if you'd asked me beforehand, owing to the fact that Angela was a minor and in violation of the law. She'd also broken another one of Hegbert's rules for proper behavior. Hegbert frowned on lawbreaking *and* drinking, and though it didn't get him going like fornication, we all knew he was deadly serious, and we assumed Jamie felt the same way. And maybe she did, but her helper instinct must have taken over. She probably took one look at Angela and thought "wounded critter" or something like that and took immediate charge of the situation. I went off and located Eric behind the bleachers, and he agreed to stand guard at the bathroom door while Jamie and I went in to tidy it up. Angela had done a marvelous job, I tell you. The puke was everywhere except the toilet. The walls, the floor, the sinks—even on the ceiling, though don't ask me how she did that. So there I was, perched on all fours, cleaning up puke at the homecoming dance in my best blue suit, which was exactly what I had wanted to avoid in the first place. And Jamie, my date, was on all fours, too, doing exactly the same thing.

I could practically hear Carey laughing a squeaky, maniacal laugh somewhere in the distance.

We ended up sneaking out the back door of the gym, keeping Angela stable by walking on either side of her. She kept asking where Lew was, but Jamie told her not to worry. She had a real soothing way of talking to Angela, though Angela was so far gone, I doubt if she even knew who was speaking. We loaded Angela into the backseat of my car, where she passed out almost immediately, although not before she'd vomited once more on the floor of the car. The smell was so awful that we had to roll down the windows to keep from gagging, and the drive to Angela's house seemed extra long. Her mother answered the door, took one look at her daughter, and brought her inside without so much as a word of thanks. I think she was embarrassed, and we really didn't have much to say to her anyway. The situation pretty much spoke for itself.

By the time we dropped her off it was ten forty-five, and we drove straight back to Jamie's. I was really worried when we got there because of the way she looked and smelled, and I said a silent prayer hoping that Hegbert wasn't awake. I didn't want to have to explain this to him. Oh, he'd probably listen to Jamie if she was the one who told him about it, but I had the sinking feeling that he'd find a way to blame me anyway.

So I walked her to the door, and we stood outside under the porchlight. Jamie crossed her arms and smiled a little, looking just as if she'd come in from an evening stroll where she'd contemplated the beauty of the world.

"Please don't tell your father about this," I said.

"I won't," she said. She kept on smiling when she finally turned my way. "I had a good time tonight. Thank you for taking me to the dance."

Here she was, covered in puke, actually thanking me for the evening. Jamie Sullivan could really drive a guy crazy sometimes.

Four

~

In the two weeks following the homecoming dance, my life pretty much returned to normal. My father was back in Washington, D.C., which made things a lot more fun around my house, primarily because I could sneak out the window again and head to the graveyard for my late night forays. I don't know what it was about the graveyard that attracted us so. Maybe it had something to do with the tombstones themselves, because as far as tombstones went, they were actually fairly comfortable to sit on.

We usually sat in a small plot where the Preston family had been buried about a hundred years ago. There were eight tombstones there, all arranged in a circle, making it easy to pass the boiled peanuts back and forth between us. One time my friends and I decided to learn what we could about the Preston family, and we went to the library to find out if anything had been written about them. I mean, if you're going to sit on someone's tombstone, you might as well know something about them, right?

It turns out that there wasn't much about the family in the historical records, though we did find out one interesting tidbit of information. Henry Preston, the father, was a one-armed lumberjack, believe it or not. Supposedly he could cut down a tree as fast as any two-armed man. Now the vision of a one-armed lumberjack is pretty vivid right off the bat, so we talked about him a lot. We used to wonder what else he could do with only one arm, and we'd spend long hours discussing how fast he could pitch a baseball or whether or not he'd be able to swim across the Intracoastal Waterway. Our conversations weren't exactly highbrow, I admit, but I enjoyed them nonetheless.

Well, Eric and me were out there one Saturday night with a couple of other friends, eating boiled peanuts and talking about Henry Preston, when Eric asked me how my "date" went with Jamie Sullivan. He and I hadn't seen much of each other since the homecoming dance because the football season was already in the playoffs and Eric had been out of town the past few weekends with the team.

"It was okay," I said, shrugging, doing my best to play it cool.

Eric playfully elbowed me in the ribs, and I grunted. He outweighed me by at least thirty pounds.

"Did you kiss her good-night?"

"No."

He took a long drink from his can of Budweiser as I answered. I don't know how he did it, but Eric never had trouble buying beer, which was strange, being that everyone in town knew how old he was.

He wiped his lips with the back of his hand, tossing me a sidelong glance.

"I would have thought that after she helped you clean the bathroom, you would have at least kissed her good-night."

"Well, I didn't."

"Did you even try?"

"No."

"Why not?"

"She's not that kind of girl," I said, and even though we all knew it was true, it still sounded like I was defending her.

Eric latched on to that like a leech.

"I think you like her," he said.

"You're full of crap," I answered, and he slapped my back, hard enough to force the breath right out of me. Hanging out with Eric usually meant that I'd have a few bruises the following day.

"Yeah, I might be full of crap," he said, winking at me, "but you're the one who's smitten with Jamie Sullivan."

I knew we were treading on dangerous ground.

"I was just using her to impress Margaret," I said. "And with all the love notes she's been sending me lately, I reckon it must have worked."

Eric laughed aloud, slapping me on the back again.

"You and Margaret—now *that's* funny . . ."

I knew I'd just dodged a major bullet, and I breathed a sigh of relief as the conversation spun off in a new direction. I joined in now and then, but I wasn't really listening to what they were saying. Instead I kept hearing this little voice inside me that made me wonder about what Eric had said.

The thing was, Jamie was probably the best date I could have had that night, especially considering how the evening turned out. Not many dates—heck, not many people, period—would have done what she did. At the same time, her being a good date didn't mean I liked her. I hadn't talked to her at all since the dance, except when I saw her in drama class, and even then it was only a few words here and there. If I liked her at all, I told myself, I would have wanted to talk to her. If I liked her, I would have offered to walk her home. If I liked her, I would have wanted to bring her to Cecil's Diner for a basket of hushpuppies and some RC cola. But I didn't want to do any of those things. I really didn't. In my mind, I'd already served my penance.

The next day, Sunday, I was in my room, working on my application to UNC. In addition to the transcripts from my high school and other personal information, they required five essays of the usual type. If you could meet one person in history, who would that person be and why? Name the most significant influence in your life and why you feel that way. What do you look for in a role model and why? The essay questions were fairly predictable—our English teacher had told us what to expect—and I'd already worked on a couple of variations in class as homework.

English was probably my best subject. I'd never received anything lower than an A since I first started school, and I was glad the emphasis for the application process was on writing. If it had been on math, I might have been in trouble, especially if it included

those algebra questions that talked about the two
trains leaving an hour apart, traveling in opposite
directions at forty miles an hour, etc. It wasn't that I
was bad in math—I usually pulled at least a C—but
it didn't come naturally to me, if you know what I
mean.

Anyway, I was writing one of my essays when the
phone rang. The only phone we had was located in
the kitchen, and I had to run downstairs to grab the
receiver. I was breathing so loudly that I couldn't make
out the voice too well, though it sounded like Angela. I
immediately smiled to myself. Even though she'd been
sick all over the place and I'd had to clean it up, she was
actually pretty fun to be around most of the time. And
her dress really had been something, at least for the
first hour. I figured she was probably calling to thank
me or even to get together for a barbecue sandwich and
hushpuppies or something.

"Landon?"

"Oh, hey," I said, playing it cool, "what's going on?"

There was a short pause on the other end.

"How are you?"

It was then that I suddenly realized I wasn't speaking to Angela. Instead it was Jamie, and I almost
dropped the phone. I can't say that I was happy about
hearing from her, and for a second I wondered who had
given her my phone number before I realized it was
probably in the church records.

"Landon?"

"I'm fine," I finally blurted out, still in shock.

"Are you busy?" she asked.

"Sort of."

"Oh...I see...," she said, trailing off. She paused again.

"Why are you calling me?" I asked.

It took her a few seconds to get the words out.

"Well...I just wanted to know if you wouldn't mind coming by a little later this afternoon."

"Coming by?"

"Yes. To my house."

"Your house?" I didn't even try to disguise the growing surprise in my voice. Jamie ignored it and went on.

"There's something I want to talk to you about. I wouldn't ask if it wasn't important."

"Can't you just tell me over the phone?"

"I'd rather not."

"Well, I'm working on my college application essays all afternoon," I said, trying to get out of it.

"Oh...well...like I said, it's important, but I suppose I can talk to you Monday at school..."

With that, I suddenly realized that she wasn't going to let me off the hook and that we'd end up talking one way or the other. My brain suddenly clicked through the scenarios as I tried to figure out which one I should do—talk to her where my friends would see us or talk at her house. Though neither option was particularly good, there was something in the back of my mind, reminding me that she'd helped me out when I'd really needed it, and the least I could do was to listen to what she had to say. I may be irresponsible, but I'm a *nice* irresponsible, if I do say so myself.

Of course, that didn't mean everyone else had to know about it.

"No," I said, "today is fine…"

We arranged to meet at five o'clock, and the rest of the afternoon ticked by slowly, like the drips from Chinese water torture. I left my house twenty minutes early, so I'd have plenty of time to get there. My house was located near the waterfront in the historic part of town, just a few doors down from where Blackbeard used to live, overlooking the Intracoastal Waterway. Jamie lived on the other side of town, across the railroad tracks, so it would take me about that long to get there.

It was November, and the temperature was finally cooling down. One thing I really liked about Beaufort was the fact that the springs and falls lasted practically forever. It might get hot in the summer or snow once every six years, and there might be a cold spell that lasted a week or so in January, but for the most part all you needed was a light jacket to make it through the winter. Today was one of those perfect days—mid-seventies without a cloud in the sky.

I made it to Jamie's house right on time and knocked on her door. Jamie answered it, and a quick peek inside revealed that Hegbert wasn't around. It wasn't quite warm enough for sweet tea or lemonade, and we sat in the chairs on the porch again, without anything to drink. The sun was beginning to lower itself in the sky, and there wasn't anyone on the street. This time I didn't have to move my chair. It hadn't been moved since the last time I'd been there.

"Thank you for coming, Landon," she said. "I know you're busy, but I appreciate your taking the time to do this."

"So, what's so important?" I said, wanting to get this over with as quickly as possible.

Jamie, for the first time since I'd known her, actually looked nervous as she sat with me. She kept bringing her hands together and pulling them apart.

"I wanted to ask you a favor," she said seriously.

"A favor?"

She nodded.

At first I thought she was going to ask me to help her decorate the church, like she'd mentioned at homecoming, or maybe she needed me to use my mother's car to bring some stuff to the orphans. Jamie didn't have her license, and Hegbert needed their car anyway, being that there was always a funeral or something he had to go to. But it still took a few seconds for her to get the words out.

She sighed, her hands coming together again.

"I'd like to ask you if you wouldn't mind playing Tom Thornton in the school play," she said.

Tom Thornton, like I said before, was the man in search of the music box for his daughter, the one who meets the angel. Except for the angel, it was far and away the most important role.

"Well...I don't know," I said, confused. "I thought Eddie Jones was going to be Tom. That's what Miss Garber told us."

Eddie Jones was a lot like Carey Dennison, by the way. He was really skinny, with pimples all over his face, and he usually talked to you with his eyes all squinched up. He had a nervous tic, and he couldn't help but squinch his eyes whenever he got nervous, which was practically all the time. He'd probably end up spouting his lines like a psychotic blind man if you put him in front of a crowd. To make things worse, he had a stutter, too, and it took him a long time to say anything at all. Miss Garber had given him the role because he'd been the only one who offered to do it, but even then it was obvious she didn't want him, either. Teachers were human, too, but she didn't have much of an option, since no one else had come forward.

"Miss Garber didn't say that exactly. What she said was that Eddie could have the role if no one else tried out for it."

"Can't someone else do it instead?"

But there really wasn't anyone else, and I knew it. Because of Hegbert's requirement that only seniors perform, the play was in a bind that year. There were about fifty senior boys at the high school, twenty-two of whom were on the football team, and with the team still in the running for the state title, none of them would have the time to go to the rehearsals. Of the thirty or so who were left, more than half were in the band and they had after-school practice as well. A quick calculation showed that there were maybe a dozen other people who could possibly do it.

Now, I didn't want to do the play at all, and not only because I'd come to realize that drama was just about the most boring class ever invented. The thing was, I'd already taken Jamie to homecoming, and with her as the angel, I just couldn't bear the thought that I'd have to spend every afternoon with her for the next month or so. Being seen with her once was bad enough... but being seen with her every day? What would my friends say?

But I could tell this was really important to her. The simple fact that she'd asked made that clear. Jamie never asked anyone for a favor. I think deep down she suspected that no one would ever do her a favor because of who she was. The very realization made me sad.

"What about Jeff Bangert? He might do it," I offered.

Jamie shook her head. "He can't. His father's sick, and he has to work in the store after school until his father gets back on his feet."

"What about Darren Woods?"

"He broke his arm last week when he slipped on the boat. His arm is in a sling."

"Really? I didn't know that," I said, stalling, but Jamie knew what I was doing.

"I've been praying about it, Landon," she said simply, and sighed for the second time. "I'd really like this play to be special this year, not for me, but because of my father. I want it to be the best production ever. I know how much it will mean to him to see me be the angel, because this play reminds him of my mother..." She paused, collecting her thoughts. "It would be terrible if the play was a failure this year, especially since I'm involved."

She stopped again before going on, her voice becoming more emotional as she went on.

"I know Eddie would do the best he could, I really do. And I'm not embarrassed to do the play with him, I'm really not. Actually, he's a very nice person, but he told me that he's having second thoughts about doing it. Sometimes people at school can be so...so...cruel, and I don't want Eddie to be hurt. But..." She took a deep breath, "but the real reason I'm asking is because of my father. He's such a *good* man, Landon. If people make fun of his memory of my mother while I'm playing the part...well, that would break my heart. And with Eddie and me...you know what people would say."

I nodded, my lips pressed together, knowing that I would have been one of those people she was talking about. In fact, I already was. Jamie and Eddie, the dynamic duo, we called them after Miss Garber had announced that they'd be the ones doing the roles. The very fact that it was I who had started it up made me feel terrible, almost sick to my stomach.

She straightened up a little in her seat and looked at me sadly, as if she already knew I was going to say no. I guess she didn't know how I was feeling. She went on.

"I know that challenges are always part of the Lord's plan, but I don't want to believe that the Lord is cruel, especially to someone like my father. He devotes his life to God, he gives to the community. And he's already lost his wife and has had to raise me on his own. And I love him so much for it..."

Jamie turned away, but I could see the tears in her eyes. It was the first time I'd ever seen her cry. I think part of me wanted to cry, too.

"I'm not asking you to do it for me," she said softly, "I'm really not, and if you say no, I'll still pray for you. I promise. But if you'd like to do something kind for a wonderful man who means so much to me...Will you just think about it?"

Her eyes looked like those of a cocker spaniel that had just messed on the rug. I looked down at my feet.

"I don't have to think about it," I finally said. "I'll do it."

I really didn't have a choice, did I?

Five

~~

The next day I talked to Miss Garber, went through the audition, and got the part. Eddie, by the way, wasn't upset at all. In fact, I could tell he was actually relieved about the whole thing. When Miss Garber asked him if he'd be willing to let me play the role of Tom Thornton, his face sort of relaxed right there and one of his eyes popped back open. "Y-y-yes, a-a-absolutely," he said, stuttering. "I—I—I un-un-understand." It took him practically ten seconds to get the words out.

For his generosity, however, Miss Garber gave him the role of the bum, and we knew he'd do fairly well in that role. The bum, you see, was completely mute, but the angel always knew what he was thinking. At one point in the play she has to tell the mute bum that God will always watch out for him because God especially cares for the poor and downtrodden. That was one of the tip-offs to the audience that she'd been sent from heaven. Like I said earlier, Hegbert wanted it to be real clear who offered redemption and salvation, and it certainly wasn't going to be a few rickety ghosts who just popped up out of nowhere.

Rehearsals started the next week, and we rehearsed in the classroom, because the Playhouse wouldn't open their doors for us until we'd got all the "little bugs" out of our performance. By little bugs, I mean our tendency to accidentally knock over the props. The props had been made about fifteen years ago, when the play was in its first year, by Toby Bush, a sort of roving handyman who had done a few projects for the Playhouse in the past. He was a roving handyman because he drank beer all day long while he worked, and by about two o'clock or so he'd really be flying. I guess he couldn't see straight, because he'd accidentally whack his fingers with the hammer at least once a day. Whenever that happened, he'd throw down the hammer and jump up and down, holding his fingers, cursing everyone from his mother to the devil. When he finally calmed down, he'd have another beer to soothe the pain before going back to work. His knuckles were the size of walnuts, permanently swollen from years of whacking, and no one was willing to hire him on a permanent basis. The only reason Hegbert had hired him at all was because he was far and away the lowest bidder in town.

But Hegbert wouldn't allow drinking or cursing, and Toby really didn't know how to work within such a strict environment. As a result, the work was kind of sloppy, though it wasn't obvious right off the bat. After a few years the props began to fall apart, and Hegbert took it upon himself to keep the things together. But while Hegbert was good at thumping the Bible, he wasn't too good at thumping nails, and the props had bent, rusty nails sticking out all over, poking through the plywood in so many places that we had to be careful to walk exactly where we were supposed to. If we bumped them the wrong way, we'd either cut ourselves or the props would topple over, making little nail holes all over the stage floor. After a couple of years the Playhouse stage had to be resurfaced, and though they couldn't exactly close their doors to Hegbert, they made a deal with him to be more careful in the future. That meant we had to practice in the classroom until we'd worked out the "little bugs."

Fortunately Hegbert wasn't involved with the actual production of the play, because of all his ministering duties. That role fell to Miss Garber, and the first thing she told us to do was to memorize our lines as quickly as possible. We didn't have as much time as was usually allotted for rehearsals because Thanksgiving came on the last possible day in November, and Hegbert didn't want the play to be performed too close to Christmas, so as not to interfere with "its true meaning." That left us only three weeks to get the play just right, which was about a week shorter than usual.

The rehearsals began at three o'clock, and Jamie knew all her lines the first day there, which wasn't really surprising. What was surprising was that she knew all my lines, too, as well as everyone else's. We'd be going over a scene, she'd be doing it without the script, and I'd be looking down at a stack of pages, trying to figure out what my next line should be, and whenever I looked up she had this real shiny look about her, as if waiting for a burning bush or something. The only lines I knew were the mute bum's, at least on that first day, and all of a sudden I was actually envious of Eddie, at least in that regard. This was going to be a lot of work, not exactly what I'd expected when I'd signed up for the class.

My noble feelings about doing the play had worn off by the second day of rehearsals. Even though I knew I was doing the "right thing," my friends didn't understand it at all, and they'd been riding me since they'd found out. "You're doing what?" Eric asked when he learned about it. "You're doing the play with Jamie Sullivan? Are you insane or just plain stupid?" I sort of mumbled that I had a good reason, but he wouldn't let it drop, and he told everyone around us that I had a crush on her. I denied it, of course, which just made them assume it was true, and they'd laugh all the louder and tell the next person they saw. The stories kept getting wilder, too—by lunch-time I'd heard from Sally that I was thinking of getting engaged. I actually think Sally was jealous about it. She'd had a crush on me for years, and the feeling might have been mutual except for the fact that she had a glass eye, and that was something I just couldn't ignore. Her bad eye reminded me of something you'd see stuffed into the head of a mounted owl in a tacky antique shop, and to be honest, it sort of gave me the willies.

I guess that was when I started to resent Jamie again. I know it wasn't her fault, but I was the one who was taking the arrows for Hegbert, who hadn't exactly gone out of his way the night of homecoming to make me feel welcome. I began to stumble through my lines in class for the next few days, not really even attempting to learn them, and occasionally I'd crack a joke or two, which everyone laughed at, except for Jamie and Miss Garber. After rehearsal was over I'd head home to put the play out of my mind, and I wouldn't even bother to pick up the script. Instead I'd joke with my friends about the weird things Jamie did and tell fibs about how it was Miss Garber who had forced me into the whole thing.

Jamie, though, wasn't going to let me off that easy. No, she got me right where it hurts, right smack in the old ego.

I was out with Eric on Saturday night following Beaufort's third consecutive state championship in football, about a week after rehearsals had started. We were hanging out at the waterfront outside of Cecil's Diner, eating hushpuppies and watching people cruising in their cars, when I saw Jamie walking down the street. She was still a hundred yards away, turning her head from side to side, wearing that old brown sweater again and carrying her Bible in one hand. It must have been nine o'clock or so, which was late for her to be out, and it was even stranger to see her in this part of town. I turned my back to her and pulled the collar up on my jacket, but even Margaret—who had banana pudding where her brain should have been—was smart enough to figure out who she was looking for.

"Landon, your girlfriend is here."

"She's not my girlfriend," I said. "I don't have a girlfriend."

"Your fiancée, then."

I guess she'd talked to Sally, too.

"I'm not engaged," I said. "Now knock it off."

I glanced over my shoulder to see if she'd spotted me, and I guess she had. She was walking toward us. I pretended not to notice.

"Here she comes," Margaret said, and giggled.

"I know," I said.

Twenty seconds later she said it again.

"She's still coming." I told you she was quick.

"I know," I said through gritted teeth. If it wasn't for her legs, she could almost drive you as crazy as Jamie.

I glanced around again, and this time Jamie knew I'd seen her and she smiled and waved at me. I turned away, and a moment later she was standing right beside me.

"Hello, Landon," she said to me, oblivious of my scorn. "Hello, Eric, Margaret..." She went around the group. Everyone sort of mumbled "hello" and tried not to stare at the Bible.

Eric was holding a beer, and he moved it behind his back so she wouldn't see it. Jamie could even make Eric feel guilty if she was close enough to him. They'd been neighbors at one time, and Eric had been on the receiving end of her talks before. Behind her back he called her "the Salvation Lady," in obvious reference to the Salvation Army. "She would have been a brigadier general," he liked to say. But when she was standing right in front of him, it was another story. In his mind she had an in with God, and he didn't want to be in her bad graces.

"How are you doing, Eric? I haven't seen you around much recently." She said this as if she still talked to him all the time.

He shifted from one foot to the other and looked at his shoes, playing that guilty look for all it was worth.

"Well, I haven't been to church lately," he said.

Jamie smiled that glittery smile. "Well, that's okay, I suppose, as long as it doesn't become a habit or anything."

"It won't."

Now I've heard of confession—that thing when Catholics sit behind a screen and tell the priest about all their sins—and that's the way Eric was when he was next to Jamie. For a second I thought he was going to call her "ma'am."

"You want a beer?" Margaret asked. I think she was trying to be funny, but no one laughed.

Jamie put her hand to her hair, tugging gently at her bun. "Oh...no, not really...thank you, though."

She looked directly at me with a really sweet glow, and right away I knew I was in trouble. I thought she was going to ask me off to the side or something, which to be honest I thought would turn out better, but I guess that wasn't in her plans.

"Well, you did really well this week at rehearsals," she said to me. "I know you've got a lot of lines to learn, but I'm sure you're going to get them all real soon. And I just wanted to thank you for volunteering like you did. You're a real gentleman."

"Thanks," I said, a little knot forming in my stomach. I tried to be cool, but all my friends were looking right at me, suddenly wondering if I'd been telling them the truth about Miss Garber forcing it on me and everything. I hoped they missed it.

"Your friends should be proud of you," Jamie added, putting that thought to rest.

"Oh, we are," Eric said, pouncing. "Very proud. He's a good guy, that Landon, what with his volunteering and all."

Oh no.

Jamie smiled at him, then turned back to me again, her old cheerful self. "I also wanted to tell you that if you need any help, you can come by anytime. We can sit on the porch like we did before and go over your lines if you need to."

I saw Eric mouth the words "like we did before" to Margaret. This really wasn't going well at all. By now the pit in my stomach was as big as Paul Bunyan's bowling ball.

"That's okay," I mumbled, wondering how I could squirm my way out of this. "I can learn them at home."

"Well, sometimes it helps if someone's there to read with you, Landon," Eric offered.

I told you he'd stick it to me, even though he was my friend.

"No, really," I said to him, "I'll learn the lines on my own."

"Maybe," Eric said, smiling, "you two should practice in front of the orphans, once you've got it down a little better. Sort of a dress rehearsal, you know? I'm sure they'd love to see it."

You could practically see Jamie's mind start clicking at the mention of the word *orphans.* Everyone knew what her hot button was. "Do you think so?" she asked.

Eric nodded seriously. "I'm sure of it. Landon was the one who thought of it first, but I know that if I was an orphan, I'd love something like that, even if it wasn't exactly the real thing."

"Me too," Margaret chimed in.

As they spoke, the only thing I could think about was that scene from *Julius Caesar* where Brutus stabs him in the back. *Et tu, Eric?*

"It was Landon's idea?" she asked, furrowing her brow. She looked at me, and I could tell she was still mulling it over.

But Eric wasn't about to let me off the hook that easy. Now that he had me flopping on the deck, the only thing left to do was gut me. "You'd like to do that, wouldn't you, Landon?" he said. "Helping the orphans, I mean."

It wasn't exactly something you could answer no to, was it?

"I reckon so," I said under my breath, staring at my best friend. Eric, despite the remedial classes he was in, would have been one hell of a chess player.

"Good, then, it's all settled. That's if it's okay with you, Jamie." His smile was so sweet, it could have flavored half the RC cola in the county.

"Well . . . yes, I suppose I'll have to talk to Miss Garber and the director of the orphanage, but if they say it's okay, I think it would be a fine idea."

And the thing was, you could tell she was really happy about it.

Checkmate.

*　　*　　*

The next day I spent fourteen hours memorizing my lines, cursing my friends, and wondering how my life had spun so out of control. My senior year certainly wasn't turning out the way I thought it would when it began, but if I had to perform for a bunch of orphans, I certainly didn't want to look like an idiot.

Six

The first thing we did was talk to Miss Garber about our plans for the orphans, and she thought it was a marvelous idea. That was her favorite word, by the way—*marvelous*—after she'd greeted you with "Hel-looooo." On Monday, when she realized that I knew all my lines, she said, "Marvelous!" and for the next two hours whenever I'd finish up a scene, she'd say it again. By the end of the rehearsal, I'd heard it about four zillion times.

But Miss Garber actually went our idea one better. She told the class what we were doing, and she asked if other members of the cast would be willing to do their parts as well, so that the orphans could really enjoy the whole thing. The way she asked meant that they really didn't have a choice, and she looked around the class, waiting for someone to nod so she could make it official. No one moved a muscle, except for Eddie. Somehow he'd inhaled a bug up his nose at that exact moment, and he sneezed violently. The bug flew out his nose, shot across his desk, and landed on the floor right by Norma Jean's leg. She jumped out of her chair and screamed out loud, and the people on either side of her shouted, "Eww... gross!" The rest of the class started looking around and craning their necks, trying to see what happened, and for the next ten seconds there was total pandemonium in the classroom. For Miss Garber, that was as good of an answer as she needed.

"Marvelous," she said, closing the discussion.

Jamie, meanwhile, was getting really excited about performing for the orphans. During a break in rehearsals she pulled me aside and thanked me for thinking of them. "There's no way you would know," she said almost conspiratorially, "but I've been wondering what to do for the orphanage this year. I've been praying about it for months now because I want this Christmas to be the most special one of all."

"Why is this Christmas so important?" I asked her, and she smiled patiently, as if I'd asked a question that didn't really matter.

"It just is," she said simply.

The next step was to talk it over with Mr. Jenkins, the director of the orphanage. Now I'd never met Mr. Jenkins before, being that the orphanage was in Morehead City, which was across the bridge from Beaufort, and I'd never had any reason to go there. When Jamie surprised me with the news the following day that we'd be meeting him later that evening, I was sort of worried that I wasn't dressed nice enough. I know it was an orphanage, but a guy wants to make a good impression. Even though I wasn't as excited about it as Jamie was (no one was as excited as Jamie), I didn't want to be regarded as the Grinch who ruined Christmas for the orphans, either.

Before we went to the orphanage for our meeting, we had to walk to my house to pick up my mom's car, and while there, I planned on changing into something a little nicer. The walk took about ten minutes or so, and Jamie didn't say much along the way, at least until we got to my neighborhood. The homes around mine were all large and well kept, and she asked who lived where and how old the houses were. I answered her questions without much thought, but when I opened the front door to my house, I suddenly realized how different this world was compared with her own. She had a shocked expression on her face as she looked around the living room, taking in her surroundings.

No doubt it was the fanciest home she'd ever been in. A moment later I saw her eyes travel to the paintings that lined the walls. My ancestors, so to speak. As with many southern families, my entire lineage could be traced in the dozen faces that lined the walls. She stared at them, looking for a resemblance, I think, then turned her attention to the furnishings, which still looked practically new, even after twenty years. The furniture had been handmade, assembled or carved from mahogany and cherry, and designed specifically for each room. It *was* nice, I had to admit, but it wasn't something I really thought about. To me, it was just a house. My favorite part of it was the window in my room that led to the porch on the upper level. That was my escape hatch.

I showed her around, though, giving her a quick tour of the sitting room, the library, the den, and the family room, Jamie's eyes growing wider with each new room. My mom was out on the sun porch, sipping a mint julep and reading, and heard us poking around. She came back inside to say hello.

I think I told you that every adult in town adored Jamie, and that included my mom. Even though Hegbert was always giving the kinds of sermons that had our family's name written all over them, my mom never held it against Jamie, because of how sweet she was. So they talked while I was upstairs rifling through my closet for a clean shirt and a tie. Back then boys wore ties a lot, especially when they were meeting someone in a position of authority. When I came back down the stairs fully dressed, Jamie had already told my mom about the plan.

"It's a wonderful idea," Jamie said, beaming at me. "Landon's really got a special heart."

My mom—after making sure she'd heard Jamie correctly—faced me with her eyebrows raised. She stared at me like I was an alien.

"So this was your idea?" my mom asked. Like everyone else in town, she knew Jamie didn't lie.

I cleared my throat, thinking of Eric and what I still wanted to do to him. It involved molasses and fire ants, by the way.

"Kind of," I said.

"Amazing." It was the only word she could get out. She didn't know the details, but she knew I must have been boxed into a corner to do something like this. Mothers always know stuff like that, and I could see her peering closely at me and trying to figure it out. To escape her inquisitive gaze, I checked my watch, feigned surprise, and casually mentioned to Jamie that we'd better be going. My mom got the car keys from her pocketbook and handed them to me, still giving me the once-over as we headed out the door. I breathed a sigh of relief, imagining that I'd somehow gotten away with something, but as I walked Jamie to the car, I heard my mother's voice again.

"Come on over anytime, Jamie!" my mom shouted. "You're always welcome here."

Even mothers could stick it to you sometimes.

I was still shaking my head as I got in the car.

"Your mother's a wonderful lady," Jamie said.

I started the engine. "Yeah," I said, "I guess so."

"And your house is beautiful."

"Uh-huh."

"You should count your blessings."

"Oh," I said, "I do. I'm practically the luckiest guy alive."

Somehow she didn't catch the sarcastic tone of my voice.

We got to the orphanage just about the time it was getting dark. We were a couple of minutes early, and the director was on the phone. It was an important call and he couldn't meet with us right away, so we made ourselves comfortable. We were waiting on a bench in the hallway outside his door, when Jamie turned to me. Her Bible was in her lap. I guess she wanted it for support, but then again, maybe it was just her habit.

"You did really well today," she said. "With your lines, I mean."

"Thanks," I said, feeling proud and dejected at exactly the same time. "I still haven't learned my beats, though," I offered. There was no way we could practice *those* on the porch, and I hoped she wasn't going to suggest it.

"You will. They're easy once you know all the words."

"I hope so."

Jamie smiled, and after a moment she changed the subject, sort of throwing me off track. "Do you ever think about the future, Landon?" she asked.

I was startled by her question because it sounded... so *ordinary.*

"Yeah, sure. I guess so," I answered cautiously.

"Well, what do you want to do with your life?"

I shrugged, a little wary of where she was going with this. "I don't know yet. I haven't figured that part out. I'm going to UNC next fall, at least I hope so. I have to get accepted first."

"You will," she said.

"How do you know?"

"Because I've prayed for that, too."

When she said it, I thought we were heading into a discussion about the power of prayer and faith, but Jamie tossed yet another curveball at me.

"How about after college? What do you want to do then?"

"I don't know," I said, shrugging. "Maybe I'll be a one-armed lumberjack."

She didn't think it was funny.

"I think you should become a minister," she said seriously. "I think you're good with people, and they'd respect what you have to say."

Though the concept was absolutely ridiculous, with her I just knew it came from the heart and she intended it as a compliment.

"Thanks," I said. "I don't know if I'll do that, but I'm sure I'll find something." It took a moment for me to realize that the conversation had stalled and that it was my turn to ask a question.

"How about you? What do you want to do in the future?"

Jamie turned away and got a far-off gaze in her eyes, making me wonder what she was thinking, but it vanished almost as quickly as it came.

"I want to get married," she said quietly. "And when I do, I want my father to walk me down the aisle and I want everyone I know to be there. I want the church bursting with people."

"That's all?" Though I wasn't averse to the idea of marriage, it seemed kind of silly to hope for that as your life's goal.

"Yes," she said. "That's all I want."

The way she answered made me suspect that she thought she'd end up like Miss Garber. I tried to make her feel better, even though it still seemed silly to me.

"Well, you'll get married someday. You'll meet some guy and the two of you will hit it off, and he'll ask you to marry him. And I'm sure that your father will be happy to walk you down the aisle."

I didn't mention the part about having a big crowd

in the church. I guess it was the one thing that even I couldn't imagine.

Jamie thought carefully about my answer, really pondering the way I said it, though I didn't know why.

"I hope so," she said finally.

I could tell she didn't want to talk about it anymore, don't ask me how, so I moved on to something new.

"So how long have you been coming to the orphanage?" I asked conversationally.

"Seven years now. I was ten years old the first time I came. I was younger than a lot of the kids here."

"Do you enjoy it, or does it make you sad?"

"Both. Some of the children here came from really horrible situations. It's enough to break your heart when you hear about it. But when they see you come in with some books from the library or a new game to play, their smiles just take all the sadness away. It's the greatest feeling in the world."

She practically glowed when she spoke. Though she wasn't saying it to make me feel guilty, that was exactly the way I felt. It was one of the reasons it was so hard to put up with her, but by then I was getting fairly used to it. She could twist you every way but normal, I'd come to learn.

At that moment, Mr. Jenkins opened the door and invited us in. The office looked almost like a hospital room, with black-and-white tiled floors, white walls and ceilings, a metal cabinet against the wall. Where the bed would normally have been, there was a metal desk that looked like it had been stamped off the assembly line. It was almost neurotically clean of anything personal. There wasn't a single picture or anything.

Jamie introduced me, and I shook Mr. Jenkins's hand. After we sat down, Jamie did most of the talking. They were old friends, you could see that right off, and Mr. Jenkins had given her a big hug as soon as she'd entered. After smoothing out her skirt, Jamie explained our plan. Now, Mr. Jenkins had seen the play a few years back, and he knew exactly what she was talking about almost as soon as she started. But even though Mr. Jenkins liked Jamie a lot and knew she meant well, he didn't think it was a good idea.

"I don't think it's a good idea," he said.

That's how I knew what he was thinking.

"Why not?" Jamie asked, her brow furrowed. She seemed genuinely perplexed by his lack of enthusiasm.

Mr. Jenkins picked up a pencil and started tapping it on his desk, obviously thinking about how to explain himself. In time, he put down the pencil and sighed.

"Even though it's a wonderful offer and I know you'd like to do something special, the play is about a father who eventually comes to realize how much he loves his daughter." He let that sink in for a moment and picked up the pencil again. "Christmas is hard enough around here without reminding the kids of what they're missing. I think that if the children see something like that . . ."

He didn't even have to finish. Jamie put her hands to her mouth. "Oh my," she said right away, "you're right. I hadn't thought about that."

Neither had I, to tell you the truth. But it was obvious right off the bat that Mr. Jenkins made sense.

He thanked us anyway and chatted for a while about

what he planned to do instead. "We'll have a small tree and a few gifts—something that all of them can share. You're welcome to visit Christmas Eve…"

After we said our good-byes, Jamie and I walked in silence without saying anything. I could tell she was sad. The more I hung around Jamie, the more I realized she had lots of different emotions—she wasn't always cheerful and happy. Believe it or not, that was the first time I recognized that in some ways she was just like the rest of us.

"I'm sorry it didn't work out," I said softly.

"I am, too."

She had that faraway look in her eyes again, and it was a moment before she went on.

"I just wanted to do something different for them this year. Something special that they would remember forever. I thought for sure this was it…" She sighed. "The Lord seems to have a plan that I just don't know about yet."

She was quiet for a long time, and I looked at her. Seeing Jamie feeling bad was almost worse than feeling bad because of her. Unlike Jamie, I deserved to feel bad about myself—I knew what kind of person I was. But with her…

"While we're here, do you want to stop in to see the kids?" I asked into the silence. It was the only thing I could think to do that might make her feel better. "I could wait out here while you talk to them, or go to the car if you want."

"Would you visit them with me?" she asked suddenly.

To be honest, I wasn't sure I could handle it, but I

knew she really wanted me there. And she was feeling so down that the words came out automatically.

"Sure, I'll go."

"They'll be in the rec room now. That's where they usually are at this time," she said.

We walked down the corridors to the end of the hall, where two doors opened into a good-size room. Perched in the far corner was a small television with about thirty metal folding chairs placed all around it. The kids were sitting in the chairs, crowded around it, and you could tell that only the ones in the front row had a good view of the thing.

I glanced around. In the corner was an old Ping-Pong table. The surface was cracked and dusty, the net nowhere to be seen. A couple of empty Styrofoam cups sat on top of it, and I knew it hadn't been used in months, maybe years. Along the wall next to the Ping-Pong table were a set of shelves, with a few toys here and there—blocks and puzzles, a couple of games. There weren't too many, and the few that were there looked as if they'd been in this room for a long time. Along the near walls were small individual desks piled with newspapers, scribbled on with crayons.

We stood in the doorway for just a second. We hadn't been noticed yet, and I asked what the newspapers were for.

"They don't have coloring books," she whispered, "so they use newspapers." She didn't look at me as she spoke—instead her attention was directed at the kids. She'd begun to smile again.

"Are these all the toys they have?" I asked.

She nodded. "Yes, except for the stuffed animals.

They're allowed to keep those in their rooms. This is where the rest of the things are kept."

I guess she was used to it. To me, though, the sparseness of the room made the whole thing depressing. I couldn't imagine growing up in a place like this.

Jamie and I finally walked into the room, and one of the kids turned around at the sound of our steps. He was about eight or so, with red hair and freckles, his two front teeth missing.

"Jamie!" he shouted happily when he saw her, and all of a sudden all the other heads turned. The kids ranged in age from about five to twelve, more boys than girls. After twelve they had to be sent to live with foster parents, I later learned.

"Hey, Roger," Jamie said in response, "how are you?"

With that, Roger and some of the others began to crowd around us. A few of the other kids ignored us and moved closer to the television now that there were free seats in the front row. Jamie introduced me to one of the older kids who'd come up and asked if I was her boyfriend. By his tone, I think that he had the same opinion of Jamie that most of the kids in our high school had.

"He's just a friend," she said. "But he's very nice."

Over the next hour, we visited with the children. I got a lot of questions about where I lived and whether my house was big or what kind of car I owned, and when we finally had to leave, Jamie promised that she'd be back soon. I noticed that she didn't promise I would be with her.

While we were walking back to the car, I said,

"They're a nice bunch of kids." I shrugged awkwardly. "I'm glad that you want to help them."

Jamie turned to me and smiled. She knew there wasn't much to add after that, but I could tell she was still wondering what she was going to do for them that Christmas.

Seven

By early December, just over two weeks into
rehearsals, the sky was winter dark before Miss
Garber would let us leave, and Jamie asked me if I
wouldn't mind walking her home. I don't know why
she wanted me to. Beaufort wasn't exactly a hotbed of
criminal activity back then. The only murder I'd ever
heard about had occurred six years earlier when a guy
was stabbed outside of Maurice's Tavern, which was a
hangout for people like Lew, by the way. For an hour or
so it caused quite a stir, and phone lines buzzed all over
town while nervous women wondered about the possibility of a crazed lunatic wandering the streets, preying on innocent victims. Doors were locked, guns were
loaded, men sat by the front windows, looking for anyone out of the ordinary who might be creeping down
the street. But the whole thing was over before the
night was through when the guy walked into the police
station to give himself up, explaining that it was a bar
fight that got out of hand. Evidently the victim had

welshed on a bet. The guy was charged with second-degree murder and got six years in the state penitentiary. The policemen in our town had the most boring jobs in the world, but they still liked to strut around with a swagger or sit in coffee shops while they talked about the "big crime," as if they'd cracked the case of the Lindbergh baby.

But Jamie's house was on the way to mine, and I couldn't say no without hurting her feelings. It wasn't that I liked her or anything, don't get the wrong idea, but when you've had to spend a few hours a day with someone, and you're going to continue doing that for at least another week, you don't want to do anything that might make the next day miserable for either of you.

The play was going to be performed that Friday and Saturday, and lots of people were already talking about it. Miss Garber had been so impressed by Jamie and me that she kept telling everyone it was going to be the best play the school had ever done. She had a real flair for promotion, too, we found out. We had one radio station in town, and they interviewed her over the air, not once, but twice. "It's going to be marvelous," she pronounced, "absolutely marvelous." She'd also called the newspaper, and they'd agreed to write an article about it, primarily because of the Jamie–Hegbert connection, even though everyone in town already knew about it. But Miss Garber was relentless, and just that day she'd told us the Playhouse was going to bring in extra seats to accommodate the extra-large crowd expected. The class sort of oohed and aahed, like it was a big deal or something, but then I guess it was to some of them. Remember, we had guys like Eddie in class. He probably thought that this would be the only time in his life when someone might be interested in him. The sad thing was, he was probably right.

You might think I'd be getting excited about it, too, but I really wasn't. My friends were still teasing me at school, and I hadn't had an afternoon off in what seemed like forever. The only thing that kept me going was the fact that I was doing the "right thing." I know it's not much, but frankly, it was all I had. Occasionally I even felt sort of good about it, too, though I never admitted it to anyone. I could practically imagine the angels in heaven, standing around and staring wistfully down at me with little tears filling the corners of their eyes, talking about how wonderful I was for all my sacrifices.

So I was walking her home that first night, thinking about this stuff, when Jamie asked me a question.

"Is it true you and your friends sometimes go to the graveyard at night?"

Part of me was surprised that she was even interested. Though it wasn't exactly a secret, it didn't seem like the sort of thing she'd care about at all.

"Yeah," I said, shrugging. "Sometimes."

"What do you do there, besides eat peanuts?"

I guess she knew about that, too.

"I don't know," I said. "Talk...joke around. It's just a place we like to go."

"Does it ever scare you?"

"No," I answered. "Why? Would it scare you?"

"I don't know," she said. "It might."

"Why?"

"Because I'd worry that I might do something wrong."

"We don't do anything bad there. I mean, we don't knock over the tombstones or leave our trash around," I said. I didn't want to tell her about our conversations about Henry Preston because I knew that wasn't the sort of thing Jamie would want to hear about. Last week Eric had wondered aloud how fast a guy like that could lie in bed and . . . well . . . you know.

"Do you ever just sit around and listen to the sounds?" she asked. "Like the crickets chirping, or the rustling of leaves when the wind blows? Or do you ever just lie on your backs and stare at the stars?"

Even though she was a teenager and had been for four years, Jamie didn't know the first thing about teenagers, and trying to understand teenage *boys* for her was like trying to decipher the theory of relativity.

"Not really," I said.

She nodded a little. "I think that's what I'd do if I were there, if I ever go, I mean. I'd just look around to really see the place, or sit quietly and listen."

This whole conversation struck me as strange, but I didn't press it, and we walked in silence for a few moments. And since she'd asked a little about me, I sort of felt obliged to ask her about herself. I mean, she hadn't brought up the Lord's plan or anything, so it was the least I could do.

"So, what do you do?" I asked. "Besides working with the orphans or helping critters or reading the Bible, I mean?" It sounded ridiculous, even to me, I admit, but *that's what she did*.

She smiled at me. I think she was surprised by

my question, and even more surprised at my interest in her.

"I do a lot of things. I study for my classes, I spend time with my dad. We play gin rummy now and then. Things like that."

"Do you ever just go off with friends and goof around?"

"No," she said, and I could tell by the way she answered that even to her, it was obvious that no one wanted her around much.

"I'll bet you're excited about going off to college next year," I said, changing the subject.

It took her a moment to answer.

"I don't think I'm going to go," she said matter-of-factly. Her answer caught me off guard. Jamie had some of the highest grades in our senior class, and depending on how the last semester went, she might even end up valedictorian. We had a running pool going as to how many times she would mention the Lord's plan in her speech, by the way. My bet was fourteen, being that she only had five minutes.

"What about Mount Sermon? I thought that's where you were planning to go. You'd love a place like that," I offered.

She looked at me with a twinkle in her eye. "You mean I'd fit right in there, don't you?"

Those curveballs she sometimes threw could smack you right between the eyeballs.

"I didn't mean it that way," I said quickly. "I just meant that I'd heard about how excited you were to be going there next year."

She shrugged without really answering me, and to be

honest, I didn't know what to make of it. By then we'd reached the front of her house, and we stopped on the sidewalk out front. From where I was standing, I could make out Hegbert's shadow in the living room through the curtains. The lamp was on, and he was sitting on the sofa by the window. His head was bowed, like he was reading something. I assumed it was the Bible.

"Thank you for walking me home, Landon," she said, and she glanced up at me for a moment before finally starting up the walk.

As I watched her go, I couldn't help but think that of all the times I'd ever talked to her, this was the strangest conversation we'd ever had. Despite the oddness of some of her answers, she seemed practically normal.

The next night, as I was walking her home, she asked me about my father.

"He's all right, I reckon," I said. "But he's not around much."

"Do you miss that? Not growing up with him around?"

"Sometimes."

"I miss my mom, too," she said, "even though I never even knew her."

It was the first time I'd ever considered that Jamie and I might have something in common. I let that sink in for a while.

"It must be hard for you," I said sincerely. "Even though my father's a stranger to me, at least he's still around."

She looked up at me as we walked, then faced forward again. She tugged gently at her hair again. I was beginning to notice that she did this whenever she was nervous or wasn't sure what to say.

"It is, sometimes. Don't get me wrong—I love my father with all my heart—but there are times when I wonder what it would have been like to have a mother around. I think she and I would have been able to talk about things in a way that my father and I can't."

I assumed she was talking about boys. It wasn't until later that I learned how wrong I was.

"What's it like, living with your father? Is he like how he is in church?"

"No. He's actually got a pretty good sense of humor."

"Hegbert?" I blurted out. I couldn't even imagine it.

I think she was shocked to hear me call him by his first name, but she let me off the hook and didn't respond to my comment. Instead she said, "Don't look so surprised. You'll like him, once you get to know him."

"I doubt if I'll ever get to know him."

"You never know, Landon," she said, smiling, "what the Lord's plan is."

I hated when she said things like that. With her, you just knew she talked to the Lord every day, and you never knew what the "Big Guy upstairs" had told her. She might even have a direct ticket into heaven, if you know what I mean, being as how good a person she was.

"How would I get to know him?" I asked.

She didn't answer, but she smiled to herself, as if she knew some secret that she was keeping from me. Like I said, I hated it when she did that.

The next night we talked about her Bible.

"Why do you always carry it with you?" I asked.

Now, I assumed she carried the Bible around simply because she was the minister's daughter. It wasn't that big of an assumption, given how Hegbert felt about Scripture and all. But the Bible she carried was old and the cover was kind of ratty looking, and I figured that she'd be the kind of person who would buy a new one every year or so just to help out the Bible publishing industry or to show her renewed dedication to the Lord or something.

She walked a few steps before answering.

"It was my mother's," she said simply.

"Oh..." I said it like I'd stepped on someone's pet turtle, squashing it under my shoe.

She looked at me. "It's okay, Landon. How could you have known?"

"I'm sorry I asked..."

"Don't be. You didn't mean anything by it." She paused. "My mother and father were given this Bible for their wedding, but my mom was the one who claimed it first. She read it all the time, especially whenever she was going through a hard time in her life."

I thought about the miscarriages. Jamie went on.

"She loved to read it at night, before she went to sleep, and she had it with her in the hospital when I was born. When my father found out that she had died, he carried the Bible and me out of the hospital at the same time."

"I'm sorry," I said again. Whenever someone tells you something sad, it's the only thing you can think to say, even if you've already said it before.

"It just gives me a way to...to be a part of her. Can you understand that?" She wasn't saying it sadly, just more to let me know the answer to my question. Somehow that made it worse.

After she told me the story, I thought of her growing up with Hegbert again, and I didn't really know what to say. As I was thinking about my answer, though, I heard a car blare its horn from behind us, and both Jamie and I stopped and turned around at the same time as we heard it pulling over to the side.

Eric and Margaret were in the car, Eric on the driver's side, Margaret on the side closest to us.

"Well, lookee who we have here," Eric said as he leaned over the steering wheel so that I could see his face. I hadn't told him I'd been walking Jamie home, and in the curious way that teenage minds work, this new development took priority over anything that I was feeling about Jamie's story.

"Hello, Eric. Hello, Margaret," Jamie said cheerfully.

"Walking her home, Landon?" I could see the little devil behind Eric's smile.

"Hey, Eric," I said, wishing he'd never seen me.

"It's a beautiful night for strolling, isn't it?" Eric said. I think that because Margaret was between him and Jamie, he felt a little bolder than he usually was in Jamie's presence. And there was no way he could let this opportunity pass without sticking it to me.

Jamie looked around and smiled. "Yes, it is."

Eric looked around, too, with this wistful look in his eyes before taking a deep breath. I could tell he was faking it. "Boy, it really is nice out there." He sighed and glanced toward us as he shrugged. "I'd offer you a ride, but it wouldn't be half as nice as actually walking under the stars, and I wouldn't want you two to miss it." He said this like he was doing us both a favor.

"Oh, we're almost to my house anyway," Jamie said. "I was going to offer Landon a cup of cider. Would you like to meet us there? We have plenty."

A cup of cider? At her house? She hadn't mentioned that. . . .

I put my hands in my pocket, wondering if this could get any worse.

"Oh, no . . . that's all right. We were just heading off to Cecil's Diner."

"On a school night?" she asked innocently.

"Oh, we won't be out too late," he promised, "but we should probably be going. Enjoy your cider, you two."

"Thanks for stopping to say hello," Jamie said, waving.

Eric got the car rolling again, but slowly. Jamie probably thought he was a safe driver. He really wasn't, though he was good at getting out of trouble when he'd crashed into something. I remember one time when he'd told his mother that a cow had jumped out in front of the car and that's why the grille and fender were damaged. "It happened so fast, Mom, the cow came out of nowhere. It just darted out in front of me, and I couldn't stop in time." Now, everyone knows cows don't exactly *dart* anywhere, but his mother believed him. She used to be a head cheerleader, too, by the way.

Once they'd pulled out of sight, Jamie turned to me and smiled.

"You have nice friends, Landon."

"Sure I do." Notice the careful way I phrased my answer.

After dropping Jamie off—no, I didn't stay for any

cider—I started back to my house, grumbling the whole time. By then Jamie's story had left me completely, and I could practically hear my friends laughing about me, all the way from Cecil's Diner.

See what happens when you're a nice guy?

By the next morning everyone at school knew I was walking Jamie home, and this started up a new round of speculation about the two of us. This time it was even worse than before. It was so bad that I had to spend my lunch break in the library just to get away from it all.

That night, the rehearsal was at the Playhouse. It was the last one before the show opened, and we had a lot to do. Right after school, the boys in drama class had to load all the props in the classroom into the rented truck to bring them to the Playhouse. The only problem was that Eddie and I were the only two boys, and he's not exactly the most coordinated individual in history. We'd be walking through a doorway, carrying one of the heavier items, and his Hooville body would work against him. At every critical moment when I really needed his help to balance the load, he'd stumble over some dust or an insect on the floor, and the weight of the prop would come crashing down on my fingers, pinching them against the doorjamb in the most painful way possible.

"S-s-sorry," he'd say. "D-d-did . . . th-th-that hurt?"

I'd stifle the curses rising in my throat and bite out, "Just don't do it again."

But he couldn't stop himself from stumbling around any more than he could stop the rain from falling. By the time we'd finished loading and unloading everything, my fingers looked like Toby's, the roving handyman. And the worst thing was, I didn't even get a chance to eat before rehearsal started. Moving the props had taken three hours, and we didn't finish setting them up until a few minutes before everyone else arrived to begin. With everything else that had happened that day, suffice it to say I was in a pretty bad mood.

I ran through my lines without even thinking about them, and Miss Garber didn't say the word *marvelous* all night long. She had this concerned look in her eyes afterward, but Jamie simply smiled and told her not to worry, that everything was going to be all right. I knew Jamie was just trying to make things better for me, but when she asked me to walk her home, I told her no. The Playhouse was in the middle of town, and to walk her home, I'd have to walk a good distance out of my way. Besides, I didn't want to be seen again doing it. But Miss Garber had overheard Jamie's request and she said, very firmly, that I'd be glad to do it. "You two can talk about the play," she said. "Maybe you can work out the kinks." By kinks, of course, she meant me specifically.

So once more I ended up walking Jamie home, but she could tell I wasn't really in the mood to talk because I walked a little bit in front of her, my hands in my pockets, without even really turning back to see whether she was following. It went this way for the first few minutes, and I hadn't said a word to her.

"You're not in a very good mood, are you?" she finally asked. "You didn't even try tonight."

"You don't miss a thing, do you?" I said sarcastically without looking at her.

"Maybe I can help," she offered. She said it kind of happily, which made me even a little angrier.

"I doubt it," I snapped.

"Maybe if you told me what was wrong—"

I didn't let her finish.

"Look," I said, stopping, turning to face her. "I've just spent all day hauling crap, I haven't eaten since lunch, and now I have to trek a mile out of my way to make sure you get home, when we both know you don't even need me to do it."

It was the first time I'd ever raised my voice to her. To tell you the truth, it felt kind of good. It had been building up for a long time. Jamie was too surprised to respond, and I went on.

"And the only reason I'm doing this is because of your father, who doesn't even like me. This whole thing is dumb, and I wish I had never agreed to do it."

"You're just saying this because you're nervous about the play—"

I cut her off with a shake of my head. Once I got on a roll, it was sometimes hard for me to stop. I could take her optimism and cheerfulness only so long, and today wasn't the day to push me too far.

"Don't you get it?" I said, exasperated. "I'm not nervous about the play, I just don't want to be here. I don't want to walk you home, I don't want my friends to keep talking about me, and I don't want to spend time with you. You keep acting like we're friends, but we're not. We're not anything. I just want the whole thing to be over so I can go back to my normal life."

She looked hurt by my outburst, and to be honest, I couldn't blame her.

"I see," was all she said. I waited for her to raise her voice at me, to defend herself, to make her case again, but she didn't. All she did was look toward the ground. I think part of her wanted to cry, but she didn't, and I finally stalked away, leaving her standing by herself. A moment later, though, I heard her start moving, too. She was about five yards behind me the rest of the way to her house, and she didn't try to talk to me again until she started up the walkway. I was already moving down the sidewalk when I heard her voice.

"Thank you for walking me home, Landon," she called out.

I winced as soon as she said it. Even when I was mean to her face and said the most spiteful things, she could find some reason to thank me. She was just that kind of girl, and I think I actually hated her for it.

Or rather, I think, I hated myself.

Eight

The night of the play was cool and crisp, the sky absolutely clear without a hint of clouds. We had to arrive an hour early, and I'd been feeling pretty bad all day about the way I'd talked to Jamie the night before. She'd never been anything but nice to me, and I knew that I'd been a jerk. I saw her in the hallways between classes, and I wanted to go up to apologize to her for what I'd said, but she'd sort of slip back into the crowd before I got the chance.

She was already at the Playhouse by the time I finally arrived, and I saw her talking to Miss Garber and Hegbert, off to one side, over by the curtains. Everyone was in motion, working off nervous energy, but she seemed strangely lethargic. She hadn't put on her costume yet—she was supposed to wear a white, flowing dress to give that angelic appearance—and she was still wearing the same sweater she'd worn at school. Despite my trepidation at how she might react, I walked up to the three of them.

"Hey, Jamie," I said. "Hello, Reverend...Miss Garber."

Jamie turned to me.

"Hello, Landon," she said quietly. I could tell she'd been thinking about the night before, too, because she didn't smile at me like she always did when she saw me. I asked if I could talk to her alone, and the two of us excused ourselves. I could see Hegbert and Miss Garber watching us as we took a few steps off to the side, out of hearing distance.

I glanced around the stage nervously.

"I'm sorry about those things I said last night," I began. "I know they probably hurt your feelings, and I was wrong to have said them."

She looked at me, as if wondering whether to believe me.

"Did you mean those things you said?" she finally asked.

"I was just in a bad mood, that's all. I get sort of wound up sometimes." I knew I hadn't really answered her question.

"I see," she said. She said it as she had the night before, then turned toward the empty seats in the audience. Again she had that sad look in her eyes.

"Look," I said, reaching for her hand, "I promise to make it up to you." Don't ask me why I said it—it just seemed like the right thing to do at that moment.

For the first time that night, she began to smile.

"Thank you," she said, turning to face me.

"Jamie?"

Jamie turned. "Yes, Miss Garber?"

"I think we're about ready for you." Miss Garber was motioning with her hand.

"I've got to go," she said to me.

"I know."

"Break a leg?" I said. Wishing someone luck before a play is supposed to be bad luck. That's why everyone tells you to "break a leg."

I let go of her hand. "We both will. I promise."

After that, we had to get ready, and we went our separate ways. I headed toward the men's dressing room. The Playhouse was fairly sophisticated, considering that it was located in Beaufort, with separate dressing rooms that made us feel as if we were actual actors, as opposed to students.

My costume, which was kept at the Playhouse, was already in the dressing room. Earlier in the rehearsals we'd had our measurements taken so that they could be altered, and I was getting dressed when Eric walked in the door unannounced. Eddie was still in the dressing room, putting on his mute bum's costume, and when he saw Eric he got a look of terror in his eyes. At least once a week Eric gave him a wedgie, and Eddie kind of hightailed it out of there as fast as he could, pulling one leg up on his costume on the way out the door. Eric ignored him and sat on the dressing table in front of the mirror.

"So," Eric said with a mischievous grin on his face, "what are you going to do?"

I looked at him curiously. "What do you mean?" I asked.

"About the play, stupid. You gonna flub up your lines or something?"

I shook my head. "No."

"You gonna knock the props over?" Everyone knew about the props.

"I hadn't planned on it," I answered stoically.

"You mean you're going to do this thing straight up?"

I nodded. Thinking otherwise hadn't even occurred to me.

He looked at me for a long time, as if he were seeing someone he'd never seen before.

"I guess you're finally growing up, Landon," he said at last. Coming from Eric, I wasn't sure whether it was intended as a compliment.

Either way, though, I knew he was right.

In the play, Tom Thornton is amazed when he first sees the angel, which is why he goes around helping her as she shares Christmas with those less fortunate. The first words out of Tom's mouth are, "You're beautiful," and I was supposed to say them as if I meant them from the bottom of my heart. This was the pivotal moment in the entire play, and it sets the tone for everything else that happens afterward. The problem, however, was that I still hadn't nailed this line yet. Sure, I said the words, but they didn't come off too convincingly, seeing as I probably said the words like anyone would when looking at Jamie, with the exception of Hegbert. It was the only scene where Miss Garber had never said the word *marvelous*, so I was nervous about it. I kept trying to imagine someone else as the angel so that I could get it just right, but with all the other things I was trying to concentrate on, it kept getting lost in the shuffle.

Jamie was still in her dressing room when the curtains

finally opened. I didn't see her beforehand, but that was okay. The first few scenes didn't include her anyway—they were mainly about Tom Thornton and his relationship with his daughter.

Now, I didn't think I'd be too nervous when I stepped out on stage, being that I'd rehearsed so much, but it hits you right between the eyes when it actually happens. The Playhouse was absolutely packed, and as Miss Garber had predicted, they'd had to set up two extra rows of seats all the way across the back. Normally the place sat four hundred, but with those seats there were at least another fifty people sitting down. In addition, people were standing against the walls, packed like sardines.

As soon as I stepped on stage, everyone was absolutely quiet. The crowd, I noticed, was mainly old ladies of the blue-haired type, the kind that play bingo and drink Bloody Marys at Sunday brunch, though I could see Eric sitting with all my friends near the back row. It was downright eerie, if you know what I mean, to be standing in front of them while everyone waited for me to say something.

So I did the best I could to put it out of my mind as I did the first few scenes in the play. Sally, the one-eyed wonder, was playing my daughter, by the way, because she was sort of small, and we went through our scenes just as we'd rehearsed them. Neither of us blew our lines, though we weren't spectacular or anything. When we closed the curtains for act two, we had to quickly reset the props. This time everyone pitched in, and my fingers escaped unscathed because I avoided Eddie at all costs.

I still hadn't seen Jamie—I guess she was exempt from moving props because her costume was made of light material and would rip if she caught it on one of those nails—but I didn't have much time to think about her because of all we had to do. The next thing I knew, the curtain was opening again and I was back in Hegbert Sullivan's world, walking past storefronts and looking in windows for the music box my daughter wants for Christmas. My back was turned from where Jamie entered, but I heard the crowd collectively draw a breath as soon as she appeared on stage. I thought it was silent before, but now it went absolutely hush still. Just then, from the corner of my eye and off to the side of the stage, I saw Hegbert's jaw quivering. I readied myself to turn around, and when I did, I finally saw what it was all about.

For the first time since I'd known her, her honey-colored hair wasn't pulled into a tight bun. Instead it was hanging loosely, longer than I imagined, reaching below her shoulder blades. There was a trace of glitter in her hair, and it caught the stage lights, sparkling like a crystal halo. Set against her flowing white dress tailored exactly for her, it was absolutely amazing to behold. She didn't look like the girl I'd grown up with or the girl I'd come recently to know. She wore a touch of makeup, too—not a lot, just enough to bring out the softness of her features. She was smiling slightly, as if she were holding a secret close to her heart, just like the part called for her to do.

She looked exactly like an angel.

I know my jaw dropped a little, and I just stood there looking at her for what seemed like a long time, shocked into silence, until I suddenly remembered that I had a line I had to deliver. I took a deep breath, then slowly let it out.

"You're beautiful," I finally said to her, and I think everyone in the whole auditorium, from the blue-haired ladies in front to my friends in the back row, knew that I actually meant it.

I'd nailed that line for the very first time.

Nine

To say that the play was a smashing success was to put it mildly. The audience laughed and the audience cried, which is pretty much what they were supposed to do. But because of Jamie's presence, it really became something special—and I think everyone in the cast was as shocked as I was at how well the whole thing had come off. They all had that same look I did when I first saw her, and it made the play that much more powerful when they were performing their parts. We finished the first performance without a hitch, and the next evening even more people showed up, if you can believe it. Even Eric came up to me afterward and congratulated me, which after what he'd said to me before was somewhat of a surprise.

"The two of you did good," he said simply. "I'm proud of you, buddy."

While he said it, Miss Garber was crying out, "Marvelous!" to anyone who would listen to her or who just happened to be walking past, repeating it over and over so much that I kept on hearing it long after I went to bed that night. I looked for Jamie after we'd pulled the curtains closed for the final time, and spotted her off to the side, with her father. He had tears in his eyes—it was the first time I'd ever seen him cry—and Jamie went into his arms, and they held each other for a long time. He was stroking her hair and whispering, "My angel," to her while her eyes were closed, and even I felt myself choking up.

The "right thing," I realized, wasn't so bad after all.

After they finally let go of each other, Hegbert proudly motioned for her to visit with the rest of the cast, and she got a boatload of congratulations from everyone backstage. She knew she'd done well, though she kept on telling people she didn't know what all the fuss was about. She was her normal cheerful self, but with her looking so pretty, it came across in a totally different way. I stood in the background, letting her have her moment, and I'll admit there was a part of me that felt like old Hegbert. I couldn't help but be happy for her, and a little proud as well. When she finally saw me standing off to one side, she excused herself from the others and walked over, finally stopping when she was close.

Looking up at me, she smiled. "Thank you, Landon, for what you did. You made my father very happy."

"You're welcome," I said, meaning it.

The strange thing was, when she said it, I realized that Hegbert would be driving her home, and for once I wished that I would have had the opportunity to walk her there.

The following Monday was our last week of school before Christmas break, and finals were scheduled in every class. In addition, I had to finish my application for UNC, which I'd sort of been putting off because of all the rehearsals. I planned on hitting the books pretty hard that week, then doing the application at night before I went to bed. Even so, I couldn't help but think about Jamie.

Jamie's transformation during the play had been startling, to say the least, and I assumed it had signaled a change in her. I don't know why I thought that way, but I did, and so I was amazed when she showed up our first morning back dressed like her usual self: brown sweater, hair in a bun, plaid skirt, and all.

One look was all it took, and I couldn't help but feel sorry for her. She'd been regarded as normal— even special—over the weekend, or so it had seemed, but she'd somehow let it slip away. Oh, people were a little nicer to her, and the ones who hadn't talked to her yet told her what a good job she'd done, too, but I could tell right off that it wasn't going to last. Attitudes forged since childhood are hard to break, and part of me wondered if it might even get worse for her after this. Now that people actually knew she could look normal, they might even become more heartless.

I wanted to talk to her about my impressions, I really did, but I was planning to do so after the week was over. Not only did I have a lot to do, but I wanted a little time to think of the best way to tell her. To be honest, I was still feeling a little guilty about the things I'd said to her on our last walk home, and it wasn't just because the play had turned out great. It had more to do with the fact that in all our time together, Jamie had never once been anything but kind, and I knew that I'd been wrong.

I didn't think she wanted to talk to me, either, to tell you the truth. I knew she could see me hanging out with my friends at lunch while she sat off in the corner, reading her Bible, but she never made a move toward us. But as I was leaving school that day, I heard her voice behind me, asking me if I wouldn't mind walking her home. Even though I wasn't ready to tell her yet about my thoughts, I agreed. For old times' sake, you see.

A minute later Jamie got down to business.

"Do you remember those things you said on our last walk home?" she asked.

I nodded, wishing she hadn't brought it up.

"You promised to make it up to me," she said.

For a moment I was confused. I thought I'd done that already with my performance in the play. Jamie went on.

"Well, I've been thinking about what you could do," she continued without letting me get a word in edgewise, "and this is what I've come up with."

She asked if I wouldn't mind gathering the pickle jars and coffee cans she'd set out in businesses all over town early in the year. They sat on the counters, usually near the cash registers, so that people could drop their loose change in. The money was to go to the orphans. Jamie never wanted to ask people straight out for the money, she wanted them to give voluntarily. That, in her mind, was the Christian thing to do.

I remembered seeing the containers in places like Cecil's Diner and the Crown Theater. My friends and I used to toss paper clips and slugs in there when the cashiers weren't looking, since they sounded sort of like a coin being dropped inside, then we'd chuckle to ourselves about how we were putting something over on Jamie. We used to joke about how she'd open one of her cans, expecting something good because of the weight, and she'd dump it out and find nothing but slugs and paper clips. Sometimes, when you remember the things you used to do, it makes you wince, and that's exactly what I did.

Jamie saw the look on my face.

"You don't have to do it," she said, obviously disappointed. "I was just thinking that since Christmas is coming up so quickly and I don't have a car, it'll simply take me too long to collect them all . . ."

"No," I said cutting her off, "I'll do it. I don't have much to do anyway."

So that's what I did starting Wednesday, even though I had tests to study for, even with that application needing to be finished. Jamie had given me a list of every place she'd placed a can, and I borrowed my mom's car and started at the far end of town the following day. She'd put out about sixty cans in all, and I figured that it would take only a day to collect them all. Compared to putting them out, it would be a piece of cake. It had taken Jamie almost six weeks to do because she'd first had to find sixty empty jars and cans and then she could put out only two or three a day since she didn't have a car and could carry only so many at a time. When I started out, I felt sort of funny about being the one who picked up the cans and jars, being that it was Jamie's project, but I kept telling myself that Jamie had asked me to help.

I went from business to business, collecting the cans and jars, and by end of the first day I realized it was going to take a little longer than I'd thought. I'd picked up only about twenty containers or so, because I'd forgotten one simple fact of life in Beaufort. In a small town like this, it was impossible to simply run inside and grab the can without chatting with the proprietor or saying hello to someone else you might recognize. It just wasn't done. So I'd sit there while some guy would be talking about the marlin he'd hooked last fall, or they'd ask me how school was going and mention that they needed a hand unloading a few boxes in the back, or maybe they wanted my opinion on whether they should move the magazine rack over to the other side of the store. Jamie, I knew, would have been good at this, and I tried to act like I thought she would want me to. It was her project after all.

To keep things moving, I didn't stop to check the take in between the businesses. I just dumped one jar or can into the next, combining them as I went along. By the end of the first day all the change was packed in two large jars, and I carried them up to my room. I saw a few bills through the glass—not too many—but I wasn't actually nervous until I emptied the contents onto my floor and saw that the change consisted primarily of pennies. Though there weren't nearly as many slugs or paper clips as I'd thought there might be, I was still disheartened when I counted up the money. There was $20.32. Even in 1958 that wasn't a lot of money, especially when divided among thirty kids.

I didn't get discouraged, though. Thinking that it was a mistake, I went out the next day, hauled a few dozen boxes, and chatted with another twenty proprietors while I collected cans and jars. The take: $23.89.

The third day was even worse. After counting up the money, even I couldn't believe it. There was only $11.52. Those were from the businesses down by the waterfront, where the tourists and teenagers like me hung out. We were really something, I couldn't help but think.

Seeing how little had been collected in all—$55.73—made me feel awful, especially considering that the jars had been out for almost a whole year and that I myself had seen them countless times. That night I was supposed to call Jamie to tell her the amount I'd collected, but I just couldn't do it. She'd told me how she'd wanted something extra special this year, and this wasn't going to do it—even I knew that. Instead I lied to her and told her that I wasn't going to count the total until the two of us could do it together, because it was her project, not mine. It was just too depressing. I promised to bring over the money the following afternoon, after school let out. The next day was December 21, the shortest day of the year. Christmas was only four days away.

"Landon," she said to me after counting it up, "this is a miracle!"

"How much is there?" I asked. I knew exactly how much it was.

"There's almost two hundred and forty-seven dollars here!" She was absolutely joyous as she looked up at me. Since Hegbert was home, I was allowed to sit in the living room, and that's where Jamie had counted the money. It was stacked in neat little piles all over the floor, almost all quarters and dimes. Hegbert was in the kitchen at the table, writing his sermon, and even he turned his head when he heard the sound of her voice.

"Do you think that's enough?" I asked innocently.

Little tears were coming down her cheeks as she looked around the room, still not believing what she was seeing right in front of her. Even after the play, she hadn't been nearly this happy. She looked right at me.

"It's...wonderful," she said, smiling. There was more emotion than I'd ever heard in her voice before. "Last year, I only collected seventy dollars."

"I'm glad it worked out better this year," I said through the lump that had formed in my throat. "If you hadn't placed those jars out so early in the year, you might not have collected nearly as much."

I know I was lying, but I didn't care. For once, it was the right thing to do.

I didn't help Jamie pick out the toys—I figured she'd know better what the kids would want anyway—but she'd insisted that I go with her to the orphanage on Christmas Eve so that I could be there when the children opened their gifts. "Please, Landon," she'd said, and with her being so excited and all, I just didn't have the heart to turn her down.

So three days later, while my father and mother were at a party at the mayor's house, I dressed in a houndstooth jacket and my best tie and walked to my mom's car with Jamie's present beneath my arm. I'd spent my last few dollars on a nice sweater because that was all

I could think to get her. She wasn't exactly the easiest person to shop for.

I was supposed to be at the orphanage at seven, but the bridge was up near the Morehead City port, and I had to wait until an outbound freighter slowly made its way down the channel. As a result, I arrived a few minutes late. The front door was already locked by that time, and I had to pound on it until Mr. Jenkins finally heard me. He fiddled through his set of keys until he found the right one, and a moment later he opened the door. I stepped inside, patting my arms to ward off the chill.

"Ah...you're here," he said happily. "We've been waiting for you. C'mon, I'll take you to where everyone is."

He led me down the hall to the rec room, the same place I'd been before. I paused for just a moment to exhale deeply before finally heading in.

It was even better than I'd imagined.

In the center of the room I saw a giant tree, decorated with tinsel and colored lights and a hundred different handmade ornaments. Beneath the tree, spread in all directions, were wrapped gifts of every size and shape. They were piled high, and the children were on the floor, sitting close together in a large semicircle. They were dressed in their best clothes, I assumed—the boys wore navy blue slacks and white collared shirts, while the girls had on navy skirts and long-sleeved blouses. They all looked as if they'd cleaned up before the big event, and most of the boys had had their hair cut.

On the table beside the door, there was a bowl of punch and platters of cookies, shaped like Christmas

trees and sprinkled with green sugar. I could see some
adults sitting with the children; a few of the smaller
kids were sitting on the adults' laps, their faces rapt
with attention as they listened to " 'Twas the Night
Before Christmas."

I didn't see Jamie, though, at least not right off the
bat. It was her voice that I recognized first. She was the
one reading the story, and I finally located her. She was
sitting on the floor in front of the tree with her legs bent
beneath her.

To my surprise, I saw that tonight her hair hung
loosely, just as it had the night of the play. Instead of
the old brown cardigan I'd seen so many times, she was
wearing a red V-neck sweater that somehow accentu-
ated the color of her light blue eyes. Even without spar-
kles in her hair or a long white flowing dress, the sight
of her was arresting. Without even noticing it, I'd been
holding my breath, and I could see Mr. Jenkins smiling at me out of the corner of my eye. I exhaled and
smiled, trying to regain control.

Jamie paused only once to look up from the story.
She noticed me standing in the doorway, then went
back to reading to the children. It took her another
minute or so to finish, and when she did, she stood up
and smoothed her skirt, then walked around the children to make her way toward me. Not knowing where
she wanted me to go, I stayed where I was.

By then Mr. Jenkins had slipped away.

"I'm sorry we started without you," she said when she
finally reached me, "but the kids were just so excited."

"It's okay," I said, smiling, thinking how nice she
looked.

"I'm so glad you could come."

"So am I."

Jamie smiled and reached for my hand to lead the way. "C'mon with me," she said. "Help me hand out the gifts."

We spent the next hour doing just that, and we watched as the children opened them one by one. Jamie had shopped all over town, picking up a few things for each child in the room, individual gifts that they'd never received before. The gifts that Jamie bought weren't the only ones the children received, however—both the orphanage and the people who worked there had bought some things as well. As paper was tossed around the room in excited frenzy, there were squeals of delight everywhere. To me, at least, it seemed that all of the children had received far more than they'd expected, and they kept thanking Jamie over and over.

By the time the dust had finally settled and all the children's gifts were opened, the atmosphere began to calm down. The room was tidied up by Mr. Jenkins and a woman I'd never met, and some of the smaller children were beginning to fall asleep beneath the tree. Some of the older ones had already gone back to their rooms with their gifts, and they'd dimmed the overhead lights on the way out the door. The tree lights cast an ethereal glow as "Silent Night" played softly on a phonograph that had been set up in the corner. I was still sitting on the floor next to Jamie, who was holding a young girl who'd fallen asleep in her lap. Because of all the commotion, we hadn't really had a chance to talk, not that either of us had minded. We were both gazing up at the lights on the tree, and I wondered what

Jamie was thinking. If truth be told, I didn't know, but she had a tender look about her. I thought—no, *I knew*—she was pleased with how the evening had gone, and deep down, so was I. To this point it was the best Christmas Eve I'd ever spent.

I glanced at her. With the lights glowing on her face, she looked as pretty as anyone I'd ever seen.

"I bought you something," I finally said to her. "A gift, I mean." I spoke softly so I wouldn't wake the little girl, and I hoped it would hide the nervousness in my voice.

She turned from the tree to face me, smiling softly. "You didn't have to do that." She kept her voice low, too, and it sounded almost musical.

"I know," I said. "But I wanted to." I'd kept the gift off to one side, and I reached for it, handing the gift-wrapped package to her.

"Could you open it for me? My hands are kind of full right now." She looked down at the little girl, then back to me.

"You don't have to open it now, if you'd rather not," I said, shrugging, "it's really not that big of a deal."

"Don't be silly," she said. "I would only open it in front of you."

To clear my mind, I looked at the gift and started opening it, picking at the tape so that it wouldn't make much noise, then unwrapping the paper until I reached the box. After setting the paper off to the side, I lifted the cover and pulled out the sweater, holding it up to show her. It was brown, like the ones she usually wore. But I figured she could use a new one.

Compared with the joy I'd seen earlier, I didn't expect much of a reaction.

"See, that's all. I told you it wasn't much," I said. I hoped she wasn't disappointed in it.

"It's beautiful, Landon," she said earnestly. "I'll wear it the next time I see you. Thank you."

We sat quietly for a moment, and once again I began to look at the lights.

"I brought you something, too," Jamie finally whispered. She looked toward the tree, and my eyes followed her gaze. Her gift was still beneath the tree, partially hidden by the stand, and I reached for it. It was rectangular, flexible, and a little heavy. I brought it to my lap and held it there without even trying to open it.

"Open it," she said, looking right at me.

"You can't give this to me," I said breathlessly. I already knew what was inside, and I couldn't believe what she had done. My hands began to tremble.

"Please," she said to me with the kindest voice I'd ever heard, "open it. I want you to have it."

Reluctantly I slowly unwrapped the package. When it was finally free of the paper, I held it gently, afraid to damage it. I stared at it, mesmerized, and slowly ran my hand over the top, brushing my fingers over the well-worn leather as tears filled my eyes. Jamie reached out and rested her hand on mine. It was warm and soft.

I glanced at her, not knowing what to say.

Jamie had given me her Bible.

"Thank you for doing what you did," she whispered to me. "It was the best Christmas I've ever had."

I turned away without responding and reached off to the side where I'd set my glass of punch. The chorus of "Silent Night" was still playing, and the music filled the room. I took a sip of the punch, trying to soothe the sudden dryness in my throat. As I drank, all the times I'd spent with Jamie came flooding into my mind. I thought about the homecoming dance and what she'd done for me that night. I thought about the play and how angelic she'd looked. I thought about the times I'd walked her home and how I'd helped collect jars and cans filled with pennies for the orphans.

As these images were going through my head, my breathing suddenly went still. I looked at Jamie, then up to the ceiling and around the room, doing my best to keep my composure, then back to Jamie again. She smiled at me and I smiled at her and all I could do was wonder how I'd ever fallen in love with a girl like Jamie Sullivan.

Ten

I drove Jamie home from the orphanage later that night. At first I wasn't sure whether I should pull the old yawn move and put my arm around her shoulder, but to be honest, I didn't know exactly how she was feeling about me. Granted, she'd given me the most wonderful gift I'd ever received, and even though I'd probably never open it and read it like she did, I knew it was like giving a piece of herself away. But Jamie was the type of person who would donate a kidney to a stranger she met walking down the street, if he really needed one. So I wasn't exactly sure what to make of it.

Jamie had told me once that she wasn't a dimwit, and I guess I finally came to the conclusion that she wasn't. She may have been . . . well, different . . . but she'd figured out what I'd done for the orphans, and looking back, I think she knew even as we were sitting on the floor of her living room. When she'd called it a miracle, I guess she was talking specifically about me.

Hegbert, I remembered, came into the room as Jamie

and I were talking about it, but he really didn't have much to say. Old Hegbert hadn't been himself lately, at least as far as I could tell. Oh, his sermons were still on the money, and he still talked about the fornicators, but lately his sermons were shorter than usual, and occasionally he'd pause right in the middle of one and this strange look would come over him, kind of like he was thinking of something else, something sad.

I didn't know what to make of it, being that I really didn't know him that well. And Jamie, when she talked about him, seemed to describe someone else entirely. I could no more imagine Hegbert with a sense of humor than I could imagine two moons in the sky.

So anyway, he came into the room while we counted the money, and Jamie stood up with those tears in her eyes, and Hegbert didn't even seem to realize I was there. He told her that he was proud of her and that he loved her, but then he shuffled back to the kitchen to continue working on his sermon. He didn't even say hello. Now, I knew I hadn't exactly been the most spiritual kid in the congregation, but I still found his behavior sort of odd.

As I was thinking about Hegbert, I glanced at Jamie sitting beside me. She was looking out the window with a peaceful look on her face, kind of smiling, but far away at the same time. I smiled. Maybe she was thinking about me. My hand started scooting across the seat closer to hers, but before I reached it, Jamie broke the silence.

"Landon," she finally asked as she turned toward me, "do you ever think about God?"

I pulled my hand back.

Now, when I thought about God, I usually pictured him like those old paintings I'd seen in churches—a giant hovering over the landscape, wearing a white robe, with long flowing hair, pointing his finger or something like that—but I knew she wasn't talking about that. She was talking about the Lord's plan. It took a moment for me to answer.

"Sure," I said. "Sometimes, I reckon."

"Do you ever wonder why things have to turn out the way they do?"

I nodded uncertainly.

"I've been thinking about it a lot lately."

Even more than usual? I wanted to ask, but I didn't. I could tell she had more to say, and I stayed quiet.

"I know the Lord has a plan for us all, but sometimes, I just don't understand what the message can be. Does that ever happen to you?"

She said this as though it were something I thought about all the time.

"Well," I said, trying to bluff, "I don't think that we're meant to understand it all the time. I think that sometimes we just have to have faith."

It was a pretty good answer, I admit. I guess that my feelings for Jamie were making my brain work a little faster than usual. I could tell she was thinking about my answer.

"Yes," she finally said, "you're right."

I smiled to myself and changed the subject, since talking about God wasn't the sort of thing that made a person feel romantic.

"You know," I said casually, "it sure was nice tonight when we were sitting by the tree earlier."

"Yes, it was," she said. Her mind was still elsewhere.

"And you sure looked nice, too."

"Thank you."

This wasn't working too well.

"Can I ask you a question?" I finally said, in the hopes of bringing her back to me.

"Sure," she said.

I took a deep breath.

"After church tomorrow, and, well...after you've spent some time with your father...I mean..." I paused and looked at her. "Would you mind coming over to my house for Christmas dinner?"

Even though her face was still turned toward the window, I could see the faint outlines of a smile as soon as I'd said it.

"Yes, Landon, I would like that very much."

I sighed with relief, not believing I'd actually asked her and still wondering how all this had happened. I drove down streets where windows were decorated with Christmas lights, and through the Beaufort City Square. A couple of minutes later when I reached across the seat, I finally took hold of her hand, and to complete the perfect evening, she didn't pull it away.

When we pulled up in front of her house, the lights in the living room were still on and I could see Hegbert behind the curtains. I supposed he was waiting up because he wanted to hear how the evening went at the orphanage. Either that, or he wanted to make sure I didn't kiss his daughter on the doorstep. I knew he'd frown on that sort of thing.

I was thinking about that—what to do when we

finally said good-bye, I mean—when we got out of the car and started toward the door. Jamie was quiet and content at the same time, and I think she was happy that I'd asked her to come over the next day. Since she'd been smart enough to figure out what I'd done for the orphans, I figured that maybe she'd been smart enough to figure out the homecoming situation as well. In her mind, I think even she realized that this was the first time I'd actually asked her to join me of my own volition.

Just as we got to her steps, I saw Hegbert peek out from behind the curtains and pull his face back. With some parents, like Angela's, for instance, that meant they knew you were home and you had about another minute or so before they'd open the door. Usually that gave you both time to sort of bat your eyes at each other while each of you worked up the nerve to actually kiss. It usually took about that long.

Now I didn't know if Jamie would kiss me; in fact, I actually doubted that she would. But with her looking so pretty, with her hair down and all, and everything that had happened tonight, I didn't want to miss the opportunity if it came up. I could feel the little butter-flies already starting to form in my stomach when Hegbert opened the door.

"I heard you pull up," he said quietly. His skin was that sallow color, as usual, but he looked tired.

"Hello, Reverend Sullivan," I said dejectedly.

"Hi, Daddy," Jamie said happily a second later. "I wish you could have come tonight. It was wonderful."

"I'm so glad for you." He seemed to gather himself then and cleared his throat. "I'll give you a bit to say good night. I'll leave the door open for you."

He turned around and went back into the living room. From where he sat down, I knew he could still see us. He pretended to be reading, though I couldn't see what was in his hands.

"I had a wonderful time tonight, Landon," Jamie said.

"So did I," I answered, feeling Hegbert's eyes on me. I wondered if he knew I'd been holding her hand during the car ride home.

"What time should I come over tomorrow?" she asked.

Hegbert's eyebrow raised just a little.

"I'll come over to get you. Is five o'clock okay?"

She looked over her shoulder. "Daddy, would you mind if I visited with Landon and his parents tomorrow?"

Hegbert brought his hand to his eyes and started rubbing them. He sighed.

"If it's important to you, you can," he said.

Not the most stirring vote of confidence I'd ever heard, but it was good enough for me.

"What should I bring?" she asked. In the South it was tradition to always ask that question.

"You don't need to bring anything," I answered. "I'll pick you up at a quarter to five."

We stood there for a moment without saying anything else, and I could tell Hegbert was growing a little impatient. He hadn't turned a page of the book since we'd been standing there.

"I'll see you tomorrow," she said finally.

"Okay," I said.

She glanced down at her feet for a moment, then

back up at me. "Thank you for driving me home," she said.

With that, she turned around and walked inside. I could barely see the slight smile playing gently across her lips as she peeked around the door, just as it was about to close.

The next day I picked her up right on schedule and was pleased to see that her hair was down once more. She was wearing the sweater I'd given her, just like she'd promised.

Both my mom and dad were a little surprised when I'd asked if it would be all right if Jamie came by for dinner. It wasn't a big deal—whenever my dad was around, my mom would have Helen, our cook, make enough food for a small army.

I guess I didn't mention that earlier, about the cook, I mean. In our house we had a maid and a cook, not only because my family could afford them, but also because my mom wasn't the greatest homemaker in the world. She was all right at making sandwiches for my lunch now and then, but there'd been times when the mustard would stain her nails, and it would take her at least three or four days to get over it. Without Helen I would have grown up eating burned mashed potatoes and crunchy steak. My father, luckily, had realized this as soon as they married, and both the cook and the maid had been with us since before I was born.

Though our house was larger than most, it wasn't a palace or anything, and neither the cook nor the maid lived with us because we didn't have separate living quarters or anything like that. My father had bought

the home because of its historical value. Though it
wasn't the house where Blackbeard had once lived,
which would have been more interesting to someone
like me, it *had* been owned by Richard Dobbs Spaight,
who'd signed the Constitution. Spaight had also owned
a farm outside of New Bern, which was about forty
miles up the road, and that was where he was buried.
Our house might not have been as famous as the one
where Dobbs Spaight was buried, but it still afforded
my father some bragging rights in the halls of Congress, and whenever he walked around the garden, I
could see him dreaming about the legacy he wanted to
leave. In a way it made me sad, because no matter what
he did, he'd never top old Richard Dobbs Spaight. Historical events like signing the Constitution come along
only once every few hundred years, and no matter
how you sliced it, debating farm subsidies for tobacco
farmers or talking about the "Red influence" was never
going to cut it. Even someone like me knew that.

The house was in the *National Historic Register*—
still is, I suppose—and though Jamie had been there
once before, she was still kind of awed when she
walked inside. My mother and father were both dressed
very nicely, as was I, and my mother kissed Jamie hello
on the cheek. My mother, I couldn't help but think as I
watched her do it, had scored before I did.

We had a nice dinner, fairly formal with four
courses, though it wasn't stuffy or anything like that.
My parents and Jamie carried on the most marvelous
conversation—think Miss Garber here—and though I
tried to inject my own brand of humor, it didn't really
go over too well, at least as far as my parents were

concerned. Jamie, however, would laugh, and I took that as a good sign.

After dinner I invited Jamie to walk around the garden, even though it was winter and nothing was in bloom. After putting on our coats, we stepped outside into the chilled winter air. I could see our breaths coming out in little puffs.

"Your parents are wonderful people," she said to me. I guess she hadn't taken Hegbert's sermons to heart.

"They're nice," I responded, "in their own way. My mom's especially sweet." I said this not only because it was true, but also because it was the same thing that kids said about Jamie. I hoped she would get the hint.

She stopped to look at the rosebushes. They looked like gnarled sticks, and I didn't see what her interest was in them.

"Is it true about your grandfather?" she asked me. "The stories that people tell?"

I guess she didn't get my hint.

"Yes," I said, trying not to show my disappointment.

"That's sad," she said simply. "There's more to life than money."

"I know."

She looked at me. "Do you?"

I didn't meet her eyes as I answered. Don't ask me why.

"I know that what my grandfather did was wrong."

"But you don't want to give it back, do you?"

"I've never really thought about it, to tell you the truth."

"Would you, though?"

I didn't answer right away, and Jamie turned from me. She was staring at the rosebushes with their gnarled sticks again, and I suddenly realized that she'd wanted me to say yes. It's what she would have done without thinking twice about it.

"Why do you do things like that?" I blurted out before I could stop myself, blood rushing into my cheeks. "Making me feel guilty, I mean. I wasn't the one who did it. I just happened to be born into this family."

She reached out and touched a branch. "That doesn't mean you can't undo it," she said gently, "when you get the opportunity."

Her point was clear, even to me, and deep down I knew she was right. But that decision, if it ever came, was a long way off. To my way of thinking, I had more important things on my mind. I changed the subject back to something I could relate to better.

"Does your father like me?" I asked. I wanted to know if Hegbert would allow me to see her again.

It took a moment for her to answer.

"My father," she said slowly, "worries about me."

"Don't all parents?" I asked.

She looked at her feet, then off to the side again before turning back to me.

"I think that with him, it's different from most. But my father does like you, and he knows that it makes me happy to see you. That's why he let me come over to your house for dinner tonight."

"I'm glad he did," I said, meaning it.

"So am I."

We looked at each other under the light of a waxing

crescent moon, and I almost kissed her right then, but she turned away a moment too soon and said something that sort of threw me.

"My father worries about you, too, Landon."

The way she said it—it was soft and sad at the same time—let me know that it wasn't simply because he thought I was irresponsible, or that I used to hide behind the trees and call him names, or even that I was a member of the Carter family.

"Why?" I asked.

"For the same reason that I do," she said. She didn't elaborate any further, and I knew right then that she was holding something back, something that she couldn't tell me, something that made her sad as well. But it wasn't until later that I learned her secret.

Being in love with a girl like Jamie Sullivan was without a doubt the strangest thing I'd ever been through. Not only was she a girl that I'd never thought about before this year—even though we'd grown up together—but there was something different in the whole way my feelings for her had unfolded. This wasn't like being with Angela, whom I'd kissed the first time I was ever alone with her. I still hadn't kissed Jamie. I hadn't even hugged her or taken her to Cecil's Diner or even to a movie. I hadn't done any of the things that I normally did with girls, yet somehow I'd fallen in love.

The problem was, I still didn't know how she felt about me.

Oh sure, there were some indications, and I hadn't missed them. The Bible was, of course, the biggie, but there was also the way she'd looked at me when she'd

closed the door on Christmas Eve, and she'd let me
hold her hand on the ride home from the orphanage.
To my way of thinking there was definitely something
there—I just wasn't exactly sure of how to take the
next step.

When I'd finally taken her home after Christmas
dinner, I'd asked if it would be okay if I came by from
time to time, and she'd said it would be fine. That's
exactly how she'd said it, too—"That would be fine."
I didn't take the lack of enthusiasm personally—Jamie
had a tendency to talk like an adult, and I think that's
why she got along with older people so well.

The following day I walked to her house, and the
first thing I noticed was that Hegbert's car wasn't in the
driveway. When she answered the door, I knew enough
not to ask her if I could come in.

"Hello, Landon," she said as she always did, as if it
were a surprise to see me. Again her hair was down,
and I took this as a positive sign.

"Hey, Jamie," I said casually.

She motioned to the chairs. "My father's not home,
but we can sit on the porch if you'd like…"

Don't even ask me how it happened, because I still
can't explain it. One second I was standing there in
front of her, expecting to walk to the side of the porch,
and in the next second I wasn't. Instead of moving
toward the chairs, I took a step closer to her and found
myself reaching for her hand. I took it in mine and
looked right at her, moving just a little closer. She didn't
exactly step back, but her eyes widened just a little,
and for a tiny, flickering moment I thought I'd done the
wrong thing and debated going any further. I paused

and smiled, sort of tilting my head to the side, and the next thing I saw was that she'd closed her eyes and was tilting her head, too, and that our faces were moving closer together.

It wasn't that long, and it certainly wasn't the kind of kiss you see in movies these days, but it was wonderful in its own way, and all I can remember about the moment is that when our lips first touched, I knew the memory would last forever.

Eleven

You're the first boy I've ever kissed," she said to me.

It was a few days before the new year, and Jamie and I were standing at the Iron Steamer Pier in Pine Knoll Shores. To get there, we'd had to cross the bridge that spans the Intracoastal Waterway and drive a little way down the island. Nowadays the place has some of the most expensive beach-front property in the entire state, but back then it was mainly sand dunes nestled against the Maritime National Forest.

"I figured I might have been," I said.

"Why?" she asked innocently. "Did I do it wrong?" She didn't look like she'd be too upset if I'd said yes, but it wouldn't have been the truth.

"You're a great kisser," I said, giving her hand a squeeze.

She nodded and turned toward the ocean, her eyes getting that far-off look again. She'd been doing that a lot lately. I let it go on for a while before the silence sort of got to me.

"Are you okay, Jamie?" I finally asked.

Instead of answering, she changed the subject.

"Have you ever been in love?" she asked me.

I ran my hand through my hair and gave her one of those looks. "You mean before now?"

I said it like James Dean would have, the way Eric had told me to say it if a girl ever asked me that question. Eric was pretty slick with girls.

"I'm serious, Landon," she said, tossing me a sidelong glance.

I guess Jamie had seen those movies, too. With Jamie, I'd come to realize, I always seemed to be going from high to low and back to high again in less time than it takes to swat a mosquito. I wasn't quite sure if I liked that part of our relationship yet, though to be honest, it kept me on my toes. I was still feeling off balance as I thought about her question.

"Actually, I have," I said finally.

Her eyes were still fixed on the ocean. I think she thought I was talking about Angela, but looking back, I'd realized that what I'd felt for Angela was totally different from what I was feeling right now.

"How did you know it was love?" she asked me.

I watched the breeze gently moving her hair, and I knew that it was no time to pretend I was something that I actually wasn't.

"Well," I said seriously, "you know it's love when all you want to do is spend time with the other person, and you sort of know that the other person feels the same way."

Jamie thought about my answer before smiling faintly.

"I see," she said softly. I waited for her to add something else, but she didn't, and I came to another sudden realization.

Jamie may not have been all that experienced with boys, but to tell you the truth, she was playing me like a harp.

During the next two days, for instance, she wore her hair in a bun again.

On New Year's Eve I took Jamie out to dinner. It was the very first real date she'd ever been on, and we went to a small waterfront restaurant in Morehead City, a place called Flauvin's. Flauvin's was the kind of restaurant with tablecloths and candles and five different pieces of silverware per setting. The waiters wore black and white, like butlers, and when you looked out the giant windows that completely lined the wall, you could watch moonlight reflecting off the slowly moving water.

There was a pianist and a singer, too, not every night or even every weekend, but on holidays when they thought the place would be full. I had to make reservations, and the first time I called they said they were filled, but I had my mom call them, and the next thing you knew, something had opened up. I guess the owner needed a favor from my father or something, or maybe he just didn't want to make him angry, knowing that my grandfather was still alive and all.

It was actually my mom's idea to take Jamie out someplace special. A couple of days before, on one of those days Jamie was wearing her hair in a bun, I talked to my mom about the things I was going through.

"She's all I think about, Mom," I confessed. "I mean, I know she likes me, but I don't know if she feels the same way that I do."

"Does she mean that much to you?" she asked.

"Yes," I said quietly.

"Well, what have you tried so far?"

"What do you mean?"

My mom smiled. "I mean that young girls, even Jamie, like to be made to feel special."

I thought about that for a moment, a little confused. Wasn't that what I was trying to do?

"Well, I've been going to her house every day to visit," I said.

My mom put her hand on my knee. Even though she wasn't a great homemaker and sometimes stuck it to me, like I said earlier, she really was a sweet lady.

"Going to her house is a nice thing to do, but it's not the most romantic thing there is. You should do something that will really let her know how you feel about her."

My mom suggested buying some perfume, and though I knew that Jamie would probably be happy to receive it, it didn't sound right to me. For one thing, since Hegbert didn't allow her to wear makeup—with the single exception being the Christmas play—I was sure she couldn't wear perfume. I told my mom as much, and that was when she'd suggested taking her out to dinner.

"I don't have any money left," I said to her dejectedly. Though my family was wealthy and gave me an allowance, they never gave me more if I ran through it too quickly. "It builds responsibility," my father said, explaining it once.

"What happened to your money in the bank?"

I sighed, and my mom sat in silence while I explained what I had done. When I finished, a look of quiet satisfaction crossed her face, as if she, too, knew I was finally growing up.

"Let me worry about that," she said softly. "You just find out if she'd like to go and if Reverend Sullivan will allow it. If she can, we'll find a way to make it happen. I promise."

The following day I went to the church. I knew that Hegbert would be in his office. I hadn't asked Jamie yet because I figured she would need his permission, and for some reason I wanted to be the one who asked. I guess it had to do with the fact that Hegbert hadn't exactly been welcoming me with open arms when I visited. Whenever he'd see me coming up the walkway—like Jamie, he had a sixth sense about it—he'd peek out the curtains, then quickly pull his head back behind them, thinking that I hadn't seen him. When I knocked, it would take a long time for him to answer the door, as if he had to come from the kitchen. He'd look at me for a long moment, then sigh deeply and shake his head before finally saying hello.

His door was partially open, and I saw him sitting behind his desk, spectacles propped on his nose. He was looking over some papers—they looked almost financial—and I figured he was trying to figure out the church budget for the following year. Even ministers had bills to pay.

I knocked at the door, and he looked up with interest, as if he expected another member of the congregation, then furrowed his brow when he saw that it was me.

"Hello, Reverend Sullivan," I said politely. "Do you have a moment?"

He looked even more tired than usual, and I assumed he wasn't feeling well.

"Hello, Landon," he said wearily.

I'd dressed sharply for the occasion, by the way, with a jacket and tie. "May I come in?"

He nodded slightly, and I entered the office. He motioned for me to sit in the chair across from his desk.

"What can I do for you?" he asked.

I adjusted myself nervously in the chair. "Well, sir, I wanted to ask you something."

He stared at me, studying me before he finally spoke. "Does it have to do with Jamie?" he asked.

I took a deep breath.

"Yes, sir. I wanted to ask if it would be all right with you if I took her to dinner on New Year's Eve."

He sighed. "Is that all?" he said.

"Yes, sir," I said. "I'll bring her home any time you'd need me to."

He took off his spectacles and wiped them with his handkerchief before putting them back on. I could tell he was taking a moment to think about it.

"Will your parents be joining you?" he asked.

"No, sir."

"Then I don't think that will be possible. But thank you for asking my permission first." He looked down at the papers, making it clear it was time for me to leave. I stood from my chair and started toward the door. As I was about to go, I faced him again.

"Reverend Sullivan?"

He looked up, surprised I was still there.

"I'm sorry for those things I used to do when I was younger, and I'm sorry that I didn't always treat Jamie the way she should have been treated. But from now on, things will change. I promise you that."

He seemed to look right through me. It wasn't enough.

"I love her," I said finally, and when I said it, his attention focused on me again.

"I know you do," he answered sadly, "but I don't want to see her hurt." Even though I must have been imagining it, I thought I saw his eyes begin to water.

"I wouldn't do that to her," I said.

He turned from me and looked out the window, watching as the winter sun tried to force its way through the clouds. It was a gray day, cold and bitter.

"Have her home by ten," he finally said, as though he knew he'd made the wrong decision.

I smiled and wanted to thank him, though I didn't. I could tell that he wanted to be alone. When I glanced over my shoulder on my way out the door, I was puzzled to see his face in his hands.

I asked Jamie an hour later. The first thing she said was that she didn't think she could go, but I told her that I'd already spoken to her father. She seemed surprised, and I think it had an effect on how she viewed me after that. The one thing I didn't tell her was that it looked almost as though Hegbert had been crying as I'd made my way out the door. Not only didn't I understand it completely, I didn't want her to worry. That night, though, after talking to my mom again, she provided me with a possible explanation, and to be honest, it made perfect sense to me. Hegbert must have come to the realization that his daughter was growing up and that he was slowly losing her to me. In a way, I hoped that was true.

I picked her up right on schedule. Though I hadn't asked her to wear her hair down, she'd done it for me. Silently we drove over the bridge, down the waterfront to the restaurant. When we got to the hostess stand, the owner himself appeared and walked us to our table. It was one of the better ones in the place.

It was crowded by the time we arrived, and all around us people were enjoying themselves. On New Year's people dressed fashionably, and we were the only two teenagers in the place. I didn't think we looked too out of place, though.

Jamie had never been to Flauvin's before, and it took her just a few minutes to take it all in. She seemed nervously happy, and I knew right away that my mom had made the right suggestion.

"This is wonderful," she said to me. "Thank you for asking me."

"My pleasure," I said sincerely.

"Have you been here before?"

"A few times. My mother and father like to come here sometimes when my father comes home from Washington."

She looked out the window and stared at a boat that was passing by the restaurant, its lights blazing. For a moment she seemed lost in wonder. "It's beautiful here," she said.

"So are you," I answered.

Jamie blushed. "You don't mean that."

"Yes," I said quietly, "I do."

We held hands while we waited for dinner, and Jamie and I talked about some of the things that had happened in the past few months. She laughed when we talked about the homecoming dance, and I finally admitted the reason I'd asked her in the first place. She was a good sport about it—she sort of laughed it off cheerfully—and I knew that she'd already figured it out on her own.

"Would you want to take me again?" she teased.

"Absolutely."

Dinner was delicious—we both ordered the sea bass and salads, and when the waiter finally removed our plates, the music started up. We had an hour left before I had to bring her home, and I offered her my hand.

At first we were the only ones on the floor, everyone watching us as we glided around the floor. I think they all knew how we were feeling about each other, and it reminded them of when they were young, too. I could see them smiling wistfully at us. The lights were dim, and when the singer began a slow melody, I held her close to me with my eyes closed, wondering if anything in my life had ever been this perfect and knowing at the same time that it hadn't.

I was in love, and the feeling was even more wonderful than I ever imagined it could be.

After New Year's we spent the next week and a half together, doing the things that young couples did back then, though from time to time she seemed tired and listless. We spent time down by the Neuse River, tossing stones in the water, watching the ripples while we talked, or we went to the beach near Fort Macon. Even though it was winter, the ocean the color of iron, it was something that both of us enjoyed doing. After an hour or so Jamie would ask me to take her home, and we'd hold hands in the car. Sometimes, it seemed, she would almost nod off before we even got home, while other times she would keep up a stream of chatter all the way back so that I could barely get a word in edgewise.

Of course, spending time with Jamie also meant doing the things she enjoyed as well. Though I wouldn't go to her Bible study class—I didn't want to look like an idiot in front of her—we did visit the orphanage twice more, and each time we went there, I felt more at home. Once, though, we'd had to leave early, because she was running a slight fever. Even to my untrained eyes, it was clear that her face was flushed.

We kissed again, too, though not every time we were together, and I didn't even think of trying to make it to second base. There wasn't any need to. There was something nice when I kissed her, something gentle and right, and that was enough for me. The more I did it, the more I realized that Jamie had been misunderstood her entire life, not only by me, but by everyone.

Jamie wasn't simply the minister's daughter, someone who read the Bible and did her best to help others. Jamie was also a seventeen-year-old girl with the same hopes and doubts that I had. At least, that's what I assumed, until she finally told me.

*   *   *

I'll never forget that day because of how quiet she had been, and I had the funny feeling all day long that something important was on her mind.

I was walking her home from Cecil's Diner on the Saturday before school started up again, a day blustery with a fierce, biting wind. A nor'easter had been blowing in since the previous morning, and while we walked, we'd had to stand close to each other to stay warm. Jamie had her arm looped through mine, and we were walking slowly, even more slowly than usual, and I could tell she wasn't feeling well again. She hadn't really wanted to go with me because of the weather, but I'd asked her because of my friends. It was time, I remember thinking, that they finally knew about us. The only problem, as fate would have it, was that no one else was at Cecil's Diner. As with many coastal communities, things were quiet on the waterfront in the middle of winter.

She was quiet as we walked, and I knew that she was thinking of a way to tell me something. I didn't expect her to start the conversation as she did.

"People think I'm strange, don't they," she finally said, breaking the silence.

"Who do you mean?" I asked, even though I knew the answer.

"People at school."

"No, they don't," I lied.

I kissed her cheek as I squeezed her arm a little tighter to me. She winced, and I could tell that I'd hurt her somehow.

"Are you okay?" I asked, concerned.

"I'm fine," she said, regaining her composure and keeping the subject on track. "Will you do me a favor, though?"

"Anything," I said.

"Will you promise to tell me the truth from now on? I mean always?"

"Sure," I said.

She stopped me suddenly and looked right at me. "Are you lying to me right now?"

"No," I said defensively, wondering where this was going. "I promise that from now on, I'll always tell you the truth."

Somehow, when I said it, I knew that I'd come to regret it.

We started walking again. As we moved down the street, I glanced at her hand, which was looped through mine, and I saw a large bruise just below her ring finger. I had no idea where it had come from, since it hadn't been there the day before. For a second I thought it might have been caused by me, but then I realized that I hadn't even touched her there.

"People think I'm strange, don't they?" she asked again.

My breath was coming out in little puffs.

"Yes," I finally answered. It hurt me to say it.

"Why?" She looked almost despondent.

I thought about it. "People have different reasons," I said vaguely, doing my best not to go any further.

"But why, exactly? Is it because of my father? Or is it because I try to be nice to people?"

I didn't want anything to do with this.

"I suppose," was all I could say. I felt a little queasy.

Jamie seemed disheartened, and we walked a little farther in silence.

"Do you think I'm strange, too?" she asked me.

The way she said it made me ache more than I thought it would. We were almost at her house before I stopped her and held her close to me. I kissed her, and when we pulled apart, she looked down at the ground.

I put my finger beneath her chin, lifting her head up and making her look at me again. "You're a wonderful person, Jamie. You're beautiful, you're kind, you're gentle . . . you're everything that I'd like to be. If people don't like you, or they think you're strange, then that's their problem."

In the grayish glow of a cold winter day, I could see her lower lip begin to tremble. Mine was doing the same thing, and I suddenly realized that my heart was speeding up as well. I looked in her eyes, smiling with all the feeling I could muster, knowing that I couldn't keep the words inside any longer.

"I love you, Jamie," I said to her. "You're the best thing that ever happened to me."

It was the first time I'd ever said the words to another person besides a member of my immediate family. When I'd imagined saying it to someone else, I'd somehow thought it would be hard, but it wasn't. I'd never been more sure of anything.

As soon as I said the words, though, Jamie bowed her head and started to cry, leaning her body into mine. I wrapped my arms around her, wondering what was wrong. She was thin, and I realized for the first time that my arms went all the way around her. She'd lost

weight, even in the last week and a half, and I remembered that she'd barely touched her food earlier. She
kept crying into my chest for what seemed like a long
time. I wasn't sure what to think, or even if she felt the
same way I did. Even so, I didn't regret the words. The
truth is always the truth, and I'd just promised her that
I would never lie again.

"Please don't say that," she said to me. "Please..."

"But I do," I said, thinking she didn't believe me.

She began to cry even harder. "I'm sorry," she
whispered to me through her ragged sobs. "I'm so, so
sorry..."

My throat suddenly went dry.

"Why're you sorry?" I asked, suddenly desperate to
understand what was bothering her. "Is it because of my
friends and what they'll say? I don't care anymore—
I really don't." I was reaching for anything, confused
and, yes—scared.

It took another long moment for her to stop crying,
and in time she looked up at me. She kissed me gently,
almost like the breath of a passerby on a city street, then
ran her finger over my cheek.

"You can't be in love with me, Landon," she said
through red and swollen eyes. "We can be friends, we
can see each other... but you *can't* love me."

"Why not?" I shouted hoarsely, not understanding
any of this.

"Because," she finally said softly, "I'm very sick,
Landon."

The concept was so absolutely foreign that I couldn't
comprehend what she was trying to say.

"So what? You'll take a few days..."

A sad smile crossed her face, and I knew right then what she was trying to tell me. Her eyes never left mine as she finally said the words that numbed my soul.

"I'm dying, Landon."

Twelve

❦

She had leukemia; she'd known it since last summer.

The moment she told me, the blood drained from my face and a sheaf of dizzying images fluttered through my mind. It was as though in that brief moment, time had suddenly stopped and I understood everything that had happened between us. I understood why she'd wanted me to do the play; I understood why, after we'd performed that first night, Hegbert had whispered to her with tears in his eyes, calling her his angel; I understood why he looked so tired all the time and why he fretted that I kept coming by the house. Everything became absolutely clear.

Why she wanted Christmas at the orphanage to be so special...

Why she didn't think she'd go to college...

Why she'd given me her Bible...

It all made perfect sense, and at the same time, nothing seemed to make any sense at all.

Jamie Sullivan had leukemia...

Jamie, sweet Jamie, was dying…

My Jamie…

"No, no," I whispered to her, "there has to be some mistake…"

But there wasn't, and when she told me again, my world went blank. My head started to spin, and I clung to her tightly to keep from losing my balance. On the street I saw a man and a woman, walking toward us, heads bent and their hands on their hats to keep them from blowing away. A dog trotted across the road and stopped to smell some bushes. A neighbor across the way was standing on a stepladder, taking down his Christmas lights. Normal scenes from everyday life, things I would never have noticed before, suddenly making me feel angry. I closed my eyes, wanting the whole thing to go away.

"I'm so sorry, Landon," she kept saying over and over. It was I who should have been saying it, however. I know that now, but my confusion kept me from saying anything.

Deep down, I knew it wouldn't go away. I held her again, not knowing what else to do, tears filling my eyes, trying and failing to be the rock I think she needed.

We cried together on the street for a long time, just a little way down the road from her house. We cried some more when Hegbert opened the door and saw our faces, knowing immediately that their secret was out. We cried when we told my mother later that afternoon, and my mother held us both to her bosom and sobbed so loudly that both the maid and the cook wanted to call the doctor because they thought something had happened to my father. On Sunday Hegbert made the announcement to his congregation, his face a mask of anguish and fear, and he had to be helped back to his seat before he'd even finished.

Everyone in the congregation stared in silent disbelief at the words they'd just heard, as if they were waiting for a punch line to some horrible joke that none of them could believe had been told. Then all at once, the wailing began.

We sat with Hegbert the day she told me, and Jamie patiently answered my questions. She didn't know how long she had left, she told me. No, there wasn't anything the doctors could do. It was a rare form of the disease, they'd said, one that didn't respond to available treatment. Yes, when the school year had started, she'd felt fine. It wasn't until the last few weeks that she'd started to feel its effects.

"That's how it progresses," she said. "You feel fine, and then, when your body can't keep fighting, you don't."

Stifling my tears, I couldn't help but think about the play.

"But all those rehearsals...those long days...maybe you shouldn't have—"

"Maybe," she said, reaching for my hand and cutting me off, "doing the play was the thing that kept me healthy for so long."

Later, she told me that seven months had passed since she'd been diagnosed. The doctors had given her a year, maybe less.

These days it might have been different. These days

they could have treated her. These days Jamie would probably live. But this was happening forty years ago, and I knew what that meant.

Only a miracle could save her.

"Why didn't you tell me?"

This was the one question I hadn't asked her, the one that I'd been thinking about. I hadn't slept that night, and my eyes were still swollen. I'd gone from shock to denial to sadness to anger and back again, all night long, wishing it weren't so and praying that the whole thing had been some terrible nightmare.

We were in her living room the following day, the day that Hegbert had made the announcement to the congregation. It was January 11, 1959.

Jamie didn't look as depressed as I thought she would. But then again, she'd been living with this for seven months already. She and Hegbert had been the only ones to know, and neither of them had trusted even me. I was hurt by that and frightened at the same time.

"I'd made a decision," she explained to me, "that it would be better if I told no one, and I asked my father to do the same. You saw how people were after the services today. No one would even look me in the eye. If you had only a few months left to live, is that what you would want?"

I knew she was right, but it didn't make it any easier. I was, for the first time in my life, completely and utterly at a loss.

I'd never had anyone close to me die before, at least not anyone that I could remember. My grandmother had died when I was three, and I don't remember a single thing about her or the services that had followed or even the next few years after her passing. I'd heard stories, of course, from both my father and my grandfather, but to me that's exactly what they were. It was the same as hearing stories I might otherwise read in a newspaper about some woman I never really knew. Though my father would bring me with him when he put flowers on her grave, I never had any feelings associated with her. I felt only for the people she'd left behind.

No one in my family or my circle of friends had ever had to confront something like this. Jamie was seventeen, a child on the verge of womanhood, dying and still very much alive at the same time. I was afraid, more afraid than I'd ever been, not only for her, but for me as well. I lived in fear of doing something wrong, of doing something that would offend her. Was it okay to ever get angry in her presence? Was it okay to talk about the future anymore? My fear made talking to her difficult, though she was patient with me.

My fear, however, made me realize something else, something that made it all worse. I realized I'd never even known her when she'd been healthy. I had started to spend time with her only a few months earlier, and I'd been in love with her for only eighteen days. Those eighteen days seemed like my entire life, but now, when I looked at her, all I could do was wonder how many more days there would be.

On Monday she didn't show up for school, and I somehow knew that she'd never walk the hallways again. I'd never see her reading the Bible off by herself at lunch, I'd never see her brown cardigan moving through the crowd as she made her way to her next class. She was finished with school forever; she would never receive her diploma.

I couldn't concentrate on anything while I sat in class that first day back, listening as teacher after teacher told us what most of us had already heard. The responses were similar to those in church on Sunday. Girls cried, boys hung their heads, people told stories about her as if she were already gone. What can we do? they wondered aloud, and people looked to me for answers.

"I don't know," was all I could say.

I left school early and went to Jamie's, blowing off my classes after lunch. When I knocked at the door, Jamie answered it the way she always did, cheerfully and without, it seemed, a care in the world.

"Hello, Landon," she said, "this is a surprise." When she leaned in to kiss me, I kissed her back, though the whole thing made me want to cry.

"My father isn't home right now, but if you'd like to sit on the porch, we can."

"How can you do this?" I asked suddenly. "How can you pretend that nothing is wrong?"

"I'm not pretending that nothing is wrong, Landon. Let me get my coat and we'll sit outside and talk, okay?"

She smiled at me, waiting for an answer, and I finally nodded, my lips pressed together. She reached out and patted my arm.

"I'll be right back," she said.

I walked to the chair and sat down, Jamie emerging a moment later. She wore a heavy coat, gloves, and a hat to keep her warm. The nor'easter had passed, and the day wasn't nearly as cold as it had been over the weekend. Still, though, it was too much for her.

"You weren't in school today," I said.

She looked down and nodded. "I know."

"Are you ever going to come back?" Even though I already knew the answer, I needed to hear it from her.

"No," she said softly, "I'm not."

"Why? Are you that sick already?" I started to tear up, and she reached out and took my hand.

"No. Today I feel pretty good, actually. It's just that I want to be home in the mornings, before my father has to go to the office. I want to spend as much time with him as I can."

Before I die, she meant to say but didn't. I felt nauseated and couldn't respond.

"When the doctors first told us," she went on, "they said that I should try to lead as normal a life as possible for as long as I could. They said it would help me keep my strength up."

"There's nothing normal about this," I said bitterly.

"I know."

"Aren't you frightened?"

Somehow I expected her to say *no*, to say something wise like a grown-up would, or to explain to me that we can't presume to understand the Lord's plan.

She looked away. "Yes," she finally said, "I'm frightened all the time."

"Then why don't you act like it?"

"I do. I just do it in private."

"Because you don't trust me?"

"No," she said, "because I know you're frightened, too."

*   *   *

I began to pray for a miracle.

They supposedly happen all the time, and I'd read about them in newspapers. People regaining use of their limbs after being told they'd never walk again, or somehow surviving a terrible accident when all hope was lost. Every now and then a traveling preacher's tent would be set up outside of Beaufort, and people would go there to watch as people were healed. I'd been to a couple, and though I assumed that most of the healing was no more than a slick magic show, since I never recognized the people who were healed, there were occasionally things that even I couldn't explain. Old man Sweeney, the baker here in town, had been in the Great War fighting with an artillery unit behind the trenches, and months of shelling the enemy had left him deaf in one ear. It wasn't an act—he really couldn't hear a single thing, and there'd been times when we were kids that we'd been able to sneak off with a cinnamon roll because of it. But the preacher started praying feverishly and finally laid his hand upon the side of Sweeney's head. Sweeney screamed out loud, making people practically jump out of their seats. He had a terrified look on his face, as if the guy had touched him with a white-hot poker, but then he shook his head and looked around, uttering the words "I can hear again." Even he couldn't believe it. "The Lord," the preacher had said as Sweeney made his way back to his seat, "can do anything. The Lord listens to our prayers."

So that night I opened the Bible that Jamie had given me for Christmas and began to read. Now, I'd heard all about Bible in Sunday school or at church, but to be frank, I just remembered the highlights—the Lord sending the seven plagues so the Israelites could leave Egypt, Jonah being swallowed by a whale, Jesus walking across the water or raising Lazarus from the dead. There were other biggies, too. I knew that practically every chapter of the Bible has the Lord doing something spectacular, but I hadn't learned them all. As Christians we leaned heavily on teachings of the New Testament, and I didn't know the first things about books like Joshua or Ruth or Joel. The first night I read through Genesis, the second night I read through Exodus. Leviticus was next, followed by Numbers and then Deuteronomy. The going got a little slow during certain parts, especially as all the laws were being explained, yet I couldn't put it down. It was a compulsion that I didn't fully understand.

It was late one night, and I was tired by the time I eventually reached Psalms, but somehow I knew this was what I was looking for. Everyone has heard the Twenty-third Psalm, which starts, "The Lord is my Shepherd, I shall not want," but I wanted to read the others, since none of them were supposed to be more important than the others. After an hour I came across an underlined section that I assumed Jamie had noted because it meant something to her. This is what it said:

I cry to you, my Lord, my rock!
Do not be deaf to me, for if you are silent, I shall
go down to the pit like the rest. Hear my voice
raised in petition as I cry to you for help, as I

*raise my hands, my Lord, toward your holy of
holies.*

I closed the Bible with tears in my eyes, unable to
finish the psalm.

Somehow I knew she'd underlined it for me.

"I don't know what to do," I said numbly, staring into
the dim light of my bedroom lamp. My mom and I
were sitting on my bed. It was coming up on the end
of January, the most difficult month of my life, and I
knew that in February things would only get worse.

"I know this is hard for you," she murmured, "but
there's nothing you can do."

"I don't mean about Jamie being sick—I know there's
nothing I can do about that. I mean about Jamie and me."

My mother looked at me sympathetically. She was
worried about Jamie, but she was also worried about
me. I went on.

"It's hard for me to talk to her. All I can do when I
look at her is think about the day when I won't be able
to. So I spend all my time at school thinking about her,
wishing I could see her right then, but when I get to her
house, I don't know what to say."

"I don't know if there's anything you can say to
make her feel better."

"Then what should I do?"

She looked at me sadly and put her arm around my
shoulder. "You really love her, don't you," she said.

"With all my heart."

She looked as sad as I'd ever seen her. "What's your
heart telling you to do?"

"I don't know."

"Maybe," she said gently, "you're trying too hard to hear it."

The next day I was better with Jamie, though not much. Before I'd arrived, I'd told myself that I wouldn't say anything that might get her down—that I'd try to talk to her like I had before—and that's exactly how it went. I sat myself on her couch and told her about some of my friends and what they were doing; I caught her up on the success of the basketball team. I told her that I still hadn't heard from UNC, but that I was hopeful I'd know within the next few weeks. I told her I was looking forward to graduation. I spoke as though she'd be back to school the following week, and I knew I sounded nervous the entire time. Jamie smiled and nodded at the appropriate times, asking questions every now and then. But I think we both knew by the time I finished talking that it was the last time I would do it. It didn't feel right to either of us.

My heart was telling me exactly the same thing.

I turned to the Bible again, in the hope that it would guide me.

"How are you feeling?" I asked a couple of days later.

By now Jamie had lost more weight. Her skin was beginning to take on a slightly grayish tint, and the bones in her hands were starting to show through her skin. Again I saw bruises. We were inside her house in the living room; the cold was too much for her to bear.

Despite all this, she still looked beautiful.

"I'm doing okay," she said, smiling valiantly. "The

doctors have given me some medicine for the pain, and it seems to help a little."

I'd been coming by every day. Time seemed to be slowing down and speeding up at exactly the same time.

"Can I get anything for you?"

"No, thank you, I'm doing fine."

I looked around the room, then back at her. "I've been reading the Bible," I finally said.

"You have?" Her face lit up, reminding me of the angel I'd seen in the play. I couldn't believe that only six weeks had gone by.

"I wanted you to know."

"I'm glad you told me."

"I read the book of Job last night," I said, "where God stuck it to Job to test his faith."

She smiled and reached out to pat my arm, her hand soft on my skin. It felt nice. "You should read something else. That's not about God in one of his better moments."

"Why would he have done that to him?"

"I don't know," she said.

"Do you ever feel like Job?"

She smiled, a little twinkle in her eyes. "Sometimes."

"But you haven't lost your faith?"

"No." I knew she hadn't, but I think I was losing mine.

"Is it because you think you might get better?"

"No," she said, "it's because it's the only thing I have left."

After that, we started reading the Bible together. It somehow seemed like the right thing to do, but my heart was nonetheless telling me that there still might be something more.

At night I lay awake, wondering about it.

Reading the Bible gave us something to focus on, and all of a sudden everything started to get better between us, maybe because I wasn't as worried about doing something to offend her. What could be more right than reading the Bible? Though I didn't know nearly as much as she did about it, I think she appreciated the gesture, and occasionally when we read, she'd put her hand on my knee and simply listen as my voice filled the room.

Other times I'd be sitting beside her on the couch, looking at the Bible and watching Jamie out of the corner of my eye at the same time, and we'd come across a passage or a psalm, maybe even a proverb, and I'd ask her what she thought about it. She always had an answer, and I'd nod, thinking about it. Sometimes she asked me what I thought, and I did my best, too, though there were moments when I was bluffing and I was sure that she could tell. "Is that what it really means to you?" she'd ask, and I'd rub my chin and think about it before trying again. Sometimes, though, it was her fault when I couldn't concentrate, what with that hand on my knee and all.

One Friday night I brought her over for dinner at my house. My mom joined us for the main course, then left the table and sat in the den so that we could be alone.

It was nice there, sitting with Jamie, and I knew she felt the same way. She hadn't been leaving her house much, and this was a good change for her.

Since she'd told me about her illness, Jamie had stopped wearing her hair in a bun, and it was still as stunning as it had been the first time I'd seen her wear it down. She was looking at the china cabinet—my mom had one of those cabinets with the lights inside—when I reached across the table and took her hand.

"Thank you for coming over tonight," I said.

She turned her attention back to me. "Thanks for inviting me."

I paused. "How's your father holding up?"

Jamie sighed. "Not too well. I worry about him a lot."

"He loves you dearly, you know."

"I know."

"So do I," I said, and when I did, she looked away. Hearing me say this seemed to frighten her again.

"Will you keep coming over to my house?" she asked. "Even later, you know, when . . . ?"

I squeezed her hand, not hard, but enough to let her know that I meant what I said.

"As long as you want me to come, I'll be there."

"We don't have to read the Bible anymore, if you don't want to."

"Yes," I said softly, "I think we do."

She smiled. "You're a good friend, Landon. I don't know what I'd do without you."

She squeezed my hand, returning the favor. Sitting across from me, she looked radiant.

"I love you, Jamie," I said again, but this time she wasn't frightened. Instead our eyes met across the table, and I watched as hers began to shine. She sighed and looked away, running her hand through her hair, then turned to me again. I kissed her hand, smiling in return.

"I love you, too," she finally whispered.

They were the words I'd been praying to hear.

I don't know if Jamie told Hegbert about her feelings for me, but I somehow doubted it because his routine hadn't changed at all. It was his habit to leave the house whenever I came over after school, and this continued. I would knock at the door and listen as Hegbert explained to Jamie that he would be leaving and would be back in a couple of hours. "Okay, Daddy," I always heard her say, then I would wait for Hegbert to open the door. Once he let me in, he would open the hallway closet and silently pull out his coat and hat, buttoning the coat up all the way before he left the house. His coat was old-fashioned, black and long, like a trench coat without zippers, the kind that was fashionable earlier this century. He seldom spoke directly to me, even after he learned that Jamie and I'd begun to read the Bible together.

Though he still didn't like me in the house if he wasn't there, he nonetheless allowed me to come in. I knew that part of the reason had to do with the fact that he didn't want Jamie to get chilled by sitting on the porch, and the only other alternative was to wait at the house while I was there. But I think Hegbert needed some time alone, too, and that was the real reason for the change. He didn't talk to me about the rules of the house—I could see them in his eyes the first time he'd said I could stay. I was allowed to stay in the living room, that was all.

Jamie was still moving around fairly well, though the winter was miserable. A cold streak blew in during the last part of January that lasted nine days, followed by three straight days of drenching rain. Jamie had no interest in leaving the house in such weather, though after Hegbert had gone she and I might stand on the porch for just a couple of minutes to breathe the fresh sea air. Whenever we did this, I found myself worrying about her.

While we read the Bible, people would knock at the door at least three times every day. People were always dropping by, some with food, others just to say hello. Even Eric and Margaret came over, and though Jamie wasn't allowed to let them in, she did so anyway, and we sat in the living room and talked a little, both of them unable to meet her gaze.

They were both nervous, and it took them a couple of minutes to finally get to the point. Eric had come to apologize, he said, and he said that he couldn't imagine why all this had happened to her of all people. He also had something for her, and he set an envelope on the table, his hand shaking. His voice was choked up as he spoke, the words ringing with the most heartfelt emotion I'd ever heard him express.

"You've got the biggest heart of anyone I've ever met," he said to Jamie, his voice cracking, "and even though I took it for granted and wasn't always nice to you, I wanted to let you know how I feel. I've never been more sorry about anything in my life." He paused and swiped at the corner of his eye. "You're the best person I'll probably ever know."

As he was fighting back his tears and sniffling,

Margaret had already given in to hers and sat weeping on the couch, unable to speak. When Eric had finished, Jamie wiped tears from her cheeks, stood slowly, and smiled, opening her arms in what could only be called a gesture of forgiveness. Eric went to her willingly, finally beginning to cry openly as she gently caressed his hair, murmuring to him. The two of them held each other for a long time as Eric sobbed until he was too exhausted to cry anymore.

Then it was Margaret's turn, and she and Jamie did exactly the same thing.

When Eric and Margaret were ready to leave, they pulled on their jackets and looked at Jamie one more time, as if to remember her forever. I had no doubt that they wanted to think of her as she looked right then. In my mind she was beautiful, and I know they felt the same way.

"Hang in there," Eric said on his way out the door. "I'll be praying for you, and so will everybody else." Then he looked toward me, reached out, and patted me on the shoulder. "You too," he said, his eyes red. As I watched them leave, I knew I'd never been prouder of either of them.

Later, when we opened the envelope, we learned what Eric had done. Without telling us, he'd collected over $400 for the orphanage.

I waited for the miracle.

It hadn't come.

In early February the pills Jamie was taking were increased to help offset the heightened pain she was feeling. The higher dosages made her dizzy, and twice she fell when walking to the bathroom, one time hitting her head against the washbasin. Afterward she insisted that the doctors cut back her medicine, and with reluctance they did. Though she was able to walk normally, the pain she was feeling intensified, and sometimes even raising her arm made her grimace. Leukemia is a disease of the blood, one that runs its course throughout a person's body. There was literally no escape from it as long as her heart kept beating.

But the disease weakened the rest of her body as well, preying on her muscles, making even simple things more difficult. In the first week of February she lost six pounds, and soon walking became difficult for her, unless it was only for a short distance. That was, of course, if she could put up with the pain, which in time she couldn't. She went back to the pills again, accepting the dizziness in place of pain.

Still we read the Bible.

Whenever I visited Jamie, I would find her on the couch with the Bible already opened, and I knew that eventually her father would have to carry her there if we wanted to continue. Though she never said anything to me about it, we both knew exactly what it meant.

I was running out of time, and my heart was still telling me that there was something more I could do.

On February 14, Valentine's Day, Jamie picked out a passage from Corinthians that meant a lot to her. She told me that if she'd ever had the chance, it was the passage she'd wanted read at her wedding. This is what it said:

Love is always patient and kind. It is never jealous. Love is never boastful or conceited. It is never rude or selfish. It does not take offense and is not resentful. Love takes no pleasure in other people's sins, but delights in the truth. It is always ready to excuse, to trust, to hope, and to endure whatever comes.

Jamie was the truest essence of that very description.

Three days later, when the temperature slightly warmed, I showed her something wonderful, something I doubted she'd ever seen before, something I knew she would want to see.

Eastern North Carolina is a beautiful and special part of the country, blessed with temperate weather and, for the most part, wonderful geography. Nowhere is this more evident than Bogue Banks, an island right off the coast, near the place we grew up. Twenty-four miles long and nearly a mile wide, this island is a fluke of nature, running from east to west, hugging the coastline a half mile offshore. Those who live there can witness spectacular sunrises and sunsets every day of the year, both taking place over the expanse of the mighty Atlantic Ocean.

Jamie was bundled up heavily, standing beside me on the edge of the Iron Steamer Pier as this perfect southern evening descended. I pointed off into the distance and told her to wait. I could see our breaths, two of hers to every one of mine. I had to support Jamie as we stood there—she seemed lighter than the leaves of a tree that had fallen in autumn—but I knew that it would be worth it.

In time the glowing, cratered moon began its seeming rise from the sea, casting a prism of light across the slowly darkening water, splitting itself into a thousand different parts, each more beautiful than the last. At exactly the same moment, the sun was meeting the horizon in the opposite direction, turning the sky red and orange and yellow, as if heaven above had suddenly opened its gates and let all its beauty escape its holy confines. The ocean turned golden silver as the shifting colors reflected off it, waters rippling and sparkling with the changing light, the vision glorious, almost like the beginning of time. The sun continued to lower itself, casting its glow as far as the eye could see, before finally, slowly, vanishing beneath the waves. The moon continued its slow drift upward, shimmering as it turned a thousand different shades of yellow, each paler than the last, before finally becoming the color of the stars.

Jamie watched all this in silence, my arm tight around her, her breathing shallow and weak. As the sky was finally turning to black and the first twinkling lights began to appear in the distant southern sky, I took her in my arms. I gently kissed both her cheeks and then, finally, her lips.

"That," I said, "is exactly how I feel about you."

A week later Jamie's trips to the hospital became more regular, although she insisted that she didn't want to stay there overnight. "I want to die at home," was all she said. Since the doctors couldn't do anything for her, they had no choice but to accept her wishes.

At least for the time being.

*   *   *

"I've been thinking about the past few months," I said to her.

We were sitting in the living room, holding hands as we read the Bible. Her face was growing thinner, her hair beginning to lose its luster. Yet her eyes, those soft blue eyes, were as lovely as ever.

I don't think I'd ever seen someone as beautiful.

"I've been thinking about them, too," she said.

"You knew, from the first day in Miss Garber's class that I was going to do the play, didn't you. When you looked at me and smiled?"

She nodded. "Yes."

"And when I asked you to the homecoming dance, you made me promise that I wouldn't fall in love, but you knew that I was going to, didn't you?"

She had a mischievous gleam in her eye. "Yes."

"How did you know?"

She shrugged without answering, and we sat together for a few moments, watching the rain as it blew against the windows.

"When I told you that I prayed for you," she finally said to me, "what did you think I was talking about?"

The progression of her disease continued, speeding up as March approached. She was taking more medicine for pain, and she felt too sick to her stomach to keep down much food. She was growing weak, and it looked like she'd have to go to the hospital to stay, despite her wishes.

It was my mother and father who changed all that.

My father had driven home from Washington, hurriedly leaving although Congress was still in session.

Apparently my mother had called him and told him that if he didn't come home immediately, he might as well stay in Washington forever.

When my mother told him what was happening, my father said that Hegbert would never accept his help, that the wounds were too deep, that it was too late to do anything.

"This isn't about your family, or even about Reverend Sullivan, or anything that happened in the past," she said to him, refusing to accept his answer. "This is about our son, who happens to be in love with a little girl who needs our help. And you're going to find a way to help her."

I don't know what my father said to Hegbert or what promises he had to make or how much the whole thing eventually cost. All I know is that Jamie was soon surrounded by expensive equipment, was supplied with all the medicine she needed, and was watched by two full-time nurses while a doctor peeked in on her several times a day.

Jamie would be able to stay at home.

That night I cried on my father's shoulder for the first time in my life.

"Do you have any regrets?" I asked her. She was in her bed under the covers, a tube in her arm feeding her the medication she needed. Her face was pale, her body feather light. She could barely walk, and when she did, she now had to be supported by someone else.

"We all have regrets, Landon," she said, "but I've led a wonderful life."

"How can you say that?" I cried out, unable to hide my anguish. "With all that's happening to you?"

She squeezed my hand, her grip weak, smiling tenderly at me.

"This," she admitted as she looked around her room, "could be better."

Despite my tears I laughed, then immediately felt guilty for doing so. I was supposed to be supporting her, not the other way around. Jamie went on.

"But other than that, I've been happy, Landon. I really have. I've had a special father who taught me about God. I can look back and know that I couldn't have tried to help other people any more than I did." She paused and met my eyes. "I've even fallen in love and had someone love me back."

I kissed her hand when she said it, then held it against my cheek.

"It's not fair," I said.

She didn't answer.

"Are you still afraid?" I asked.

"Yes."

"I'm afraid, too," I said.

"I know. And I'm sorry."

"What can I do?" I asked desperately. "I don't know what I'm supposed to do anymore."

"Will you read to me?"

I nodded, though I didn't know whether I'd be able to make it through the next page without breaking down.

Please, Lord, tell me what to do!

"Mom?" I said later that night.

"Yes?"

We were sitting on the sofa in the den, the fire blazing

before us. Earlier in the day Jamie had fallen asleep while I read to her, and knowing she needed her rest, I slipped out of her room. But before I did, I kissed her gently on the cheek. It was harmless, but Hegbert had walked in as I'd done so, and I had seen the conflicting emotions in his eyes. He looked at me, knowing that I loved his daughter but also knowing that I'd broken one of the rules of his house, even an unspoken one. Had she been well, I know he would never have allowed me back inside. As it was, I showed myself to the door.

I couldn't blame him, not really. I found that spending time with Jamie sapped me of the energy to feel hurt by his demeanor. If Jamie had taught me anything over these last few months, she'd shown me that actions—not thoughts or intentions—were the way to judge others, and I knew that Hegbert would allow me in the following day. I was thinking about all this as I sat next to my mother on the sofa.

"Do you think we have a purpose in life?" I asked.

It was the first time I'd asked her such a question, but these were unusual times.

"I'm not sure I understand what you're asking," she said, frowning.

"I mean—how do you know what you're supposed to do?"

"Are you asking me about spending time with Jamie?"

I nodded, though I was still confused. "Sort of. I know I'm doing the right thing, but... something's missing. I spend time with her and we talk and read the Bible, but..."

I paused, and my mother finished my thought for me.

"You think you should be doing more?"

I nodded.

"I don't know that there's anything more you *can* do, sweetheart," she said gently.

"Then why do I feel the way I do?"

She moved a little closer on the sofa, and we watched the flames together.

"I think it's because you're frightened and you feel helpless, and even though you're trying, things continue to get harder and harder—for the both of you. And the more you try, the more hopeless things seem."

"Is there any way to stop feeling this way?"

She put her arm around me and pulled me closer. "No," she said softly, "there isn't."

The next day Jamie couldn't get out of bed. Because she was too weak now to walk even with support, we read the Bible in her room.

She fell asleep within minutes.

Another week went by and Jamie grew steadily worse, her body weakening. Bedridden, she looked smaller, almost like a little girl again.

"Jamie," I pleaded, "what can I do for you?"

Jamie, my sweet Jamie, was sleeping for hours at a time now, even as I talked to her. She didn't move at the sound of my voice; her breaths were rapid and weak.

I sat beside the bed and watched her for a long time, thinking how much I loved her. I held her hand close to my heart, feeling the boniness of her fingers. Part of me wanted to cry right then, but instead I laid her hand back down and turned to face the window.

Why, I wondered, had my world suddenly unraveled
as it had? Why had all this happened to someone like
her? I wondered if there was a greater lesson in what
was happening. Was it all, as Jamie would say, simply
part of the Lord's plan? Did the Lord want me to fall
in love with her? Or was that something of my own
volition? The longer Jamie slept, the more I felt her
presence beside me, yet the answers to these questions
were no clearer than they had been before.

Outside, the last of the morning rain had passed.
It had been a gloomy day, but now the late afternoon
sunlight was breaking through the clouds. In the cool
spring air I saw the first signs of nature coming back to
life. The trees outside were budding, the leaves waiting for just the right moment to uncoil and open themselves to yet another summer season.

On the nightstand by her bed I saw the collection
of items that Jamie held close to her heart. There were
photographs of her father, holding Jamie as a young
child and standing outside of school on her first day of
kindergarten; there was a collection of cards that children of the orphanage had sent. Sighing, I reached for
them and opened the card on top of the stack.

Written in crayon, it said simply:

Please get better soon. I miss you.

It was signed by Lydia, the girl who'd fallen asleep
in Jamie's lap on Christmas Eve. The second card
expressed the same sentiments, but what really caught
my eye was the picture that the child, Roger, had
drawn. He'd drawn a bird, soaring above a rainbow.

Choking up, I closed the card. I couldn't bear to look any further, and as I put the stack back where it had been before, I noticed a newspaper clipping, next to her water glass. I reached for the article and saw that it was about the play, published in the Sunday paper the day after we'd finished. In the photograph above the text, I saw the only picture that had ever been taken of the two of us.

It seemed so long ago. I brought the article nearer to my face. As I stared, I remembered the way I felt when I had seen her that night. Peering closely at her image, I searched for any sign that she suspected what would come to pass. I knew she did, but her expression that night betrayed none of it. Instead, I saw only a radiant happiness. In time I sighed and set aside the clipping.

The Bible still lay open where I'd left off, and although Jamie was sleeping, I felt the need to read some more. Eventually I came across another passage. This is what it said:

> I am not commanding you, but I want to test the sincerity of your love by comparing it to the earnestness of others.

The words made me choke up again, and just as I was about to cry, the meaning of it suddenly became clear.

God had finally answered me, and I suddenly knew what I had to do.

I couldn't have made it to the church any faster, even if I'd had a car. I took every shortcut I could, racing through people's backyards, jumping fences, and in one case cutting through someone's garage and out the side door. Everything I'd learned about the town growing up came into play, and although I was never a particularly good athlete, on this day I was unstoppable, propelled by what I had to do.

I didn't care how I looked when I arrived because I suspected Hegbert wouldn't care, either. When I finally entered the church, I slowed to a walk, trying to catch my breath as I made my way to the back, toward his office.

Hegbert looked up when he saw me, and I knew why he was here. He didn't invite me in, he simply looked away, back toward the window again. At home he'd been dealing with her illness by cleaning the house almost obsessively. Here, though, papers were scattered across the desk, and books were strewn about the room as if no one had straightened up for weeks. I knew that this was the place he thought about Jamie; this was the place where Hegbert came to cry.

"Reverend?" I said softly.

He didn't answer, but I went in anyway.

"I'd like to be alone," he croaked.

He looked old and beaten, as weary as the Israelites described in David's Psalms. His face was drawn, and his hair had grown thinner since December. Even more than I, perhaps, he had to keep up his spirits around Jamie, and the stress of doing so was wearing him down.

I marched right up to his desk, and he glanced at me before turning back to the window.

"Please," he said to me. His tone was defeated, as though he didn't have the strength to confront even me.

"I'd like to talk to you," I said firmly. "I wouldn't ask unless it was very important."

Hegbert sighed, and I sat in the chair I had sat in before, when I'd asked him if he would let me take Jamie out for New Year's Eve.

He listened as I told him what was on my mind.

When I was finished, Hegbert turned to me. I don't know what he was thinking, but thankfully, he didn't say no. Instead he wiped his eyes with his fingers and turned toward the window.

Even he, I think, was too shocked to speak.

Again I ran, again I didn't tire, my purpose giving me the strength I needed to go on. When I reached Jamie's house, I rushed in the door without knocking, and the nurse who'd been in her bedroom came out to see what had caused the racket. Before she could speak, I did.

"Is she awake?" I asked, euphoric and terrified at the same time.

"Yes," the nurse said cautiously. "When she woke up, she wondered where you were."

I apologized for my disheveled appearance and thanked her, then asked if she wouldn't mind leaving us alone. I walked into Jamie's room, partially closing the door behind me. She was pale, so very pale, but her smile let me know she was still fighting.

"Hello, Landon," she said, her voice faint, "thank you for coming back."

I pulled up a chair and sat next to her, taking her hand in mine. Seeing her lying there made something tighten deep in my stomach, making me almost want to cry.

"I was here earlier, but you were asleep," I said.

"I know...I'm sorry. I just can't seem to help it anymore."

"It's okay, really."

She lifted her hand slightly off the bed, and I kissed it, then leaned forward and kissed her cheek as well.

"Do you love me?" I asked her.

She smiled. "Yes."

"Do you want me to be happy?" As I asked her this, I felt my heart beginning to race.

"Of course I do."

"Will you do something for me, then?"

She looked away, sadness crossing her features. "I don't know if I can anymore," she said.

"But if you could, would you?"

I cannot adequately describe the intensity of what I was feeling at that moment. Love, anger, sadness, hope, and fear, whirling together, sharpened by the nervousness I was feeling. Jamie looked at me curiously, and my breaths became shallower. Suddenly I knew that I'd never felt as strongly for another person as I did at that moment. As I returned her gaze, this simple realization made me wish for the millionth time that I could make all this go away. Had it been possible, I would have traded my life for hers. I wanted to tell her my thoughts, but the sound of her voice suddenly silenced the emotions inside me.

"Yes," she finally said, her voice weak yet somehow still full of promise. "I would."

Finally getting control of myself, I kissed her again, then brought my hand to her face, gently running my fingers over her cheek. I marveled at the softness of her skin, the gentleness I saw in her eyes. Even now she was perfect.

My throat began to tighten again, but as I said, I knew what I had to do. Since I had to accept that it was not within my power to cure her, what I wanted to do was give her something that she'd always wanted.

It was what my heart had been telling me to do all along.

Jamie, I understood then, had already given me the answer I'd been searching for, the one my heart had needed to find. She'd told me the answer as we'd sat outside Mr. Jenkins's office, the night we'd asked him about doing the play.

I smiled softly, and she returned my affection with a slight squeeze of my hand, as if trusting me in what I was about to do. Encouraged, I leaned closer and took a deep breath. When I exhaled, these were the words that flowed with my breath.

"Will you marry me?"

Thirteen

~

When I was seventeen, my life changed forever.

As I walk the streets of Beaufort forty years later, thinking back on that year of my life, I remember everything as clearly as if it were all still unfolding before my very eyes.

I remember Jamie saying yes to my breathless question and how we both began to cry together. I remember talking to both Hegbert and my parents, explaining to them what I needed to do. They thought I was doing it only for Jamie, and all three of them tried to talk me out of it, especially when they realized that Jamie had said yes. What they didn't understand, and I had to make clear to them, was that I needed to do it for me.

I was in love with her, so deeply in love that I didn't care if she was sick. I didn't care that we wouldn't have long together. None of those things mattered to me. All I cared about was doing something that my heart had told me was the right thing to do. In my mind it was the first time God had ever spoken directly to me, and I knew with certainty that I wasn't going to disobey.

I know that some of you may wonder if I was doing it out of pity. Some of the more cynical may even wonder if I did it because she'd be gone soon anyway and I wasn't committing much. The answer to both questions is no. I would have married Jamie Sullivan no matter what happened in the future. I would have married Jamie Sullivan if the miracle I was praying for had suddenly come true. I knew it at the moment I asked her, and I still know it today.

Jamie was more than just the woman I loved. In that year Jamie helped me become the man I am today. With her steady hand she showed me how important it was to help others; with her patience and kindness she showed me what life is really all about. Her cheerfulness and optimism, even in times of sickness, was the most amazing thing I have ever witnessed.

We were married by Hegbert in the Baptist church, my father standing beside me as the best man. That was another thing she did. In the South it's a tradition to have your father beside you, but for me it's a tradition that wouldn't have had much meaning before Jamie came into my life. Jamie had brought my father and me together again; somehow she'd also managed to heal some of the wounds between our two families. After what he'd done for me and for Jamie, I knew in the end that my father was someone I could always count on, and as the years passed our relationship grew steadily stronger until his death.

Jamie also taught me the value of forgiveness and the transforming power that it offers. I realized this the day that Eric and Margaret had come to her house. Jamie held no grudges. Jamie led her life the way the Bible taught.

Jamie was not only the angel who saved Tom Thornton, she was the angel who saved us all.

Just as she'd wanted, the church was bursting with people. Over two hundred guests were inside, and more than that waited outside the doors as we were married on March 12, 1959. Because we were married on such short notice, there wasn't time to make many arrangements, and people came out of the woodwork to make the day as special as they could, simply by showing up to support us. I saw everyone I knew—Miss Garber, Eric, Margaret, Eddie, Sally, Carey, Angela, and even Lew and his grandmother—and there wasn't a dry eye in the house when the entrance music began. Although Jamie was weak and hadn't moved from her bed in two weeks, she insisted on walking down the aisle so that her father could give her away. "It's very important to me, Landon," she'd said. "It's part of my dream, remember?" Though I assumed it would be impossible, I simply nodded. I couldn't help but wonder at her faith.

I knew she planned on wearing the dress she'd worn in the Playhouse the night of the play. It was the only white dress that was available on such short notice, though I knew it would hang more loosely than it had before. While I was wondering how Jamie would look in the dress, my father laid his hand on my shoulder as we stood before the congregation.

"I'm proud of you, son."

I nodded. "I'm proud of you, too, Dad."

It was the first time I'd ever said those words to him.

My mom was in the front row, dabbing her eyes with her handkerchief when the "Wedding March" began. The doors opened and I saw Jamie, seated in her wheelchair, a nurse by her side. With all the strength she had left, Jamie stood shakily as her father supported her. Then Jamie and Hegbert slowly made their way down the aisle, while everyone in the church sat silently in wonder. Halfway down the aisle, Jamie suddenly seemed to tire, and they stopped while she caught her breath. Her eyes closed, and for a moment I didn't think she could go on. I know that no more than ten or twelve seconds elapsed, but it seemed much longer, and finally she nodded slightly. With that, Jamie and Hegbert started moving again, and I felt my heart surge with pride.

It was, I remembered thinking, the most difficult walk anyone ever had to make.

In every way, a walk to remember.

The nurse had rolled the wheelchair up front as Jamie and her father made their way toward me. When she finally reached my side, there were gasps of joy and everyone spontaneously began to clap. The nurse rolled the wheelchair into position, and Jamie sat down again, spent. With a smile I lowered myself to my knees so that I would be level with her. My father then did the same.

Hegbert, after kissing Jamie on the cheek, retrieved his Bible in order to begin the ceremony. All business now, he seemed to have abandoned his role as Jamie's father to something more distant, where he could keep his emotions in check. Yet I could see him struggling as he stood before us. He perched his glasses on his nose and opened the Bible, then looked at Jamie and me. Hegbert towered over us, and I could tell that he hadn't anticipated our being so much lower. For a moment he stood before us, almost confused, then surprisingly decided to kneel as well. Jamie smiled and reached for his free hand, then reached for mine, linking us together.

Hegbert began the ceremony in the traditional way, then read the passage in the Bible that Jamie had once pointed out to me. Knowing how weak she was, I thought he would have us recite the vows right away, but once more Hegbert surprised me. He looked at Jamie and me, then out to the congregation, then back to us again, as if searching for the right words.

He cleared his throat, and his voice rose so that everyone could hear it. This is what he said:

"As a father, I'm supposed to give away my daughter, but I'm not sure that I'm able to do this."

The congregation went silent, and Hegbert nodded at me, willing me to be patient. Jamie squeezed my hand in support.

"I can no more give Jamie away than I can give away my heart. But what I can do is to let another share in the joy that she has always given me. May God's blessings be with you both."

It was then that he set aside the Bible. He reached out, offering his hand to mine, and I took it, completing the circle.

With that he led us through our vows. My father handed me the ring my mother had helped me pick out, and Jamie gave me one as well. We slipped them on our fingers. Hegbert watched us as we did so, and when we were finally ready, he pronounced us husband and wife. I kissed Jamie softly as my mother began to cry, then held Jamie's hand in mine. In front of God and everyone else, I'd promised my love and devotion, in sickness and in health, and I'd never felt so good about anything.

It was, I remember, the most wonderful moment of my life.

It is now forty years later, and I can still remember everything from that day. I may be older and wiser, I may have lived another life since then, but I know that when my time eventually comes, the memories of that day will be the final images that float through my mind. I still love her, you see, and I've never removed my ring. In all these years I've never felt the desire to do so.

I breathe deeply, taking in the fresh spring air. Though Beaufort has changed and I have changed, the air itself has not. It's still the air of my childhood, the air of my seventeenth year, and when I finally exhale, I'm fifty-seven once more. But this is okay. I smile slightly, looking toward the sky, knowing there's one thing I still haven't told you: I now believe, by the way, that miracles can happen.

KINDRED SPIRIT

———◆———

*T*here are stories that rise from mysterious, unknown places, and others that are discovered, a gift
from someone else. This story is one of the latter. On
a cool and blustery day in the late spring of 2016, I
drove to Sunset Beach, North Carolina, one of many
small islands between Wilmington and the South
Carolina border. I parked my truck near the pier
and hiked down the beach, heading for Bird Island,
an uninhabited coastal preserve. Locals had told me
there was something I should see; perhaps, they'd even
suggested, the site would end up in one of my novels.
They told me to keep my eye out for an American flag;
when I spotted it in the distance, I'd know I was getting
close.

Not long after the flag came into view, I kept my
eyes peeled. I was to look for a mailbox called Kindred Spirit. The mailbox—planted on a pole of aging
driftwood near a saw grass–speckled dune—has
been around since 1983 and belongs to no one and

everyone. Anyone can leave a letter or postcard; any passerby can read whatever has been placed inside. Thousands of people do so every year. Over time, Kindred Spirit has been a repository of hopes and dreams in written form... and always, there are love stories to be found.

The beach was deserted. As I approached the isolated mailbox on its lonely stretch of shoreline, I could just make out a wooden bench beside it. It was the perfect resting place, an outpost of reflection.

Reaching inside the mailbox, I found two postcards, several previously opened letters, a recipe for Brunswick stew, a journal that appeared to have been written in German, and a thick manila envelope. There were pens, a pad of unused paper, and envelopes— presumably for anyone who was inspired to add their own story to the contents. Taking a seat on the bench, I perused the postcards and the recipe before turning to the letters. Almost immediately, I noticed that no one used last names. Some of the letters had first names, others had only initials, and still others were completely anonymous, which only added to the sense of mystery.

But anonymity seemed to allow for candid reflection. I read about a woman who, in the aftermath of a struggle with cancer, had met the man of her dreams at a Christian bookstore, but worried that she wasn't good enough for him. I read about a child who hoped to one day become an astronaut. There was a letter from a young man who planned to propose to his sweetheart in a hot air balloon, and still another from a man who wanted to ask his neighbor on a date but *feared rejection. There was a letter from someone recently released from prison who wanted nothing more than to start his life over. The final missive was from a man whose dog, Teddy, had recently been put to sleep. The man was still grieving, and after finishing the letter, I studied the photograph that had been tucked inside the envelope, showing a black Labrador retriever with friendly eyes and a graying muzzle. The man had signed his initials A.K., and I found myself hoping he would find a way to fill the void that Teddy's absence had left behind.*

By then, the breeze was steady and the clouds had begun to darken. A storm was rolling in. I returned the recipe, postcards, and letters to the mailbox and debated opening the manila envelope. The thickness indicated a substantial number of pages, and the last thing I wanted was to get caught in the rain as I trekked back to my truck. Flipping over the envelope as I debated, I saw that someone had printed on the back The Most Amazing Story Ever!

A plea for recognition? A challenge? Written by the author, or by someone who'd examined the contents? I wasn't sure, but how could I resist?

I opened the clasp. Inside the envelope were a dozen or so pages, photocopies of three letters, and some photocopied drawings of a man and woman who clearly looked to be in love with each other. I set those aside and reached for the story. The first line made me pause:

The destiny that matters most in anyone's life is the one concerning love.

The tone was unlike the previous letters, promising something grand, it seemed. I settled in to read. After a page or so, my curiosity became interest; after a few more pages, I couldn't put the story aside. Over the next half hour, I laughed and felt my throat tighten; I ignored the uptick in the breeze and clouds that were turning the color of charcoal. Thunder and flickers of lightning were reaching the distant edge of the island when I read the final words with a sense of wonder.

I should have left then. I could see sheets of rain marching across the waves toward me, but instead, I read the story a second time. On that reading, I was able to hear the voices of the characters with utter clarity. By the time I read the letters and examined the drawings, I could feel the idea taking shape that I might somehow find the writer and broach the possibility of turning his story into a book.

But finding that person wouldn't be easy. Most of the events had taken place long in the past—more than a quarter century earlier—and instead of names, there were only single initials. Even in the letters, the original names had been whited out before the pages were copied. There was nothing to indicate who the writer or artist might have been.

A few clues remained, however. In the part of the story dating back to 1990, there was mention of a restaurant with a deck out back and an indoor fireplace, where a cannonball allegedly salvaged from one of Blackbeard's ships sat atop the mantel. There was also reference to a cottage on an island off the North Carolina coast, within walking distance of the restaurant. And in what seemed to be the most recently written pages, the writer spoke of a construction project currently under way at a beach house, on a different island altogether. I had no idea whether the project was now finished, but I had to start somewhere. Though years had passed, I hoped the drawings would eventually help me identify the subjects. And, of course, there was also the Kindred Spirit mailbox on the beach where I sat, which played a pivotal role in the story.

By then, the sky was positively threatening and I knew I was out of time. Sliding the pages back into the manila envelope, I returned it to the mailbox and hurried to my truck. I barely beat the downpour. Had I waited another few minutes, I would have been drenched, and despite having my windshield wipers on high, I could barely see through the glass. I drove home, made myself a late lunch, and stared out the window, continuing to think about the couple that I'd read about on the pages. By evening, I knew that I wanted to go back to Kindred Spirit and examine the story again, but weather and some business travel prevented me from returning for nearly a week.

When I finally made it back, the other letters, the recipe, and the journal were there, but the manila envelope was gone. I wondered what had become of it. I was curious as to whether a stranger had been as moved by the pages as I'd been and had taken them, or if perhaps there was some sort of caretaker who occasionally purged the mailbox. Mainly, I wondered whether the author had had second thoughts about revealing the story and come to retrieve it himself.

It made me want to talk to the writer even more, but family and work kept me busy for another month, and it wasn't until June that I found time to begin my quest. I won't bore you with all the details regarding my search—it took the better part of a week, countless phone calls, visits to various chambers of commerce and county offices where building permits were recorded, and hundreds of miles on the truck. Since the first part of the story took place decades ago, some of the reference points had long since disappeared. I managed to track down the location of the restaurant—it was now a chic seafood bistro with white tablecloths—and used that as a starting point for my exploratory excursions, in order to get a sense of the area. After that, following the trail of building permits, I visited one island after the next, and on one of my many walks up and down the beach, I eventually came across the sound of hammering and a power drill—not uncommon for salted and weather-beaten homes along the coast. When I saw an older man working on a ramp that led from the top of the dune to the beach, though, I felt a sudden jolt. I remembered the drawings, and even from a distance suspected that I had found one of the characters I had read about.

Walking over, I introduced myself. Up close, I became even more certain it was him. I noted the quiet intensity I'd read about and the same observant blue eyes referenced in one of the letters. Doing the math, I figured him to be in his late sixties, which was the right age. After a bit of small talk, I asked him point-blank whether he'd written the story *that had ended up in Kindred Spirit. In response, he deliberately turned his gaze toward the ocean, saying nothing for perhaps a minute. When he turned to face me again, he said that he would answer my questions the following afternoon, but only if I was willing to lend him a hand on his construction project.*

I showed up with a tool belt early the following morning, but the tools proved unnecessary. Instead, he had me haul plywood, two-by-fours, and pressure-treated lumber from the front of the house to the back, up over the sandy dune, and onto the beach. The pile of lumber was enormous, and the sand made every load seem twice as heavy. It took me most of the day, and aside from telling me where to place the lumber, he didn't speak to me at all. He spent the day drilling and nailing and working beneath a searing early-summer sun, more interested in the quality of his work than my presence.

Shortly after I'd finished hauling the last load, he motioned for me to take a seat on the dune and opened a cooler. Filling a pair of plastic cups from a thermos inside, he handed me a cup of iced tea.

"Yeah," he finally offered. "I wrote it."

"Is it true?"

He squinted, as if evaluating me.

"Some of it," he admitted, in the accent I'd heard described in the pages. "Some might dispute the facts, but memories aren't always about facts."

I told him that I thought it might make for a fascinating book and launched into a series of passionate arguments. He listened in silence, his expression unreadable. For some reason, I felt anxious, almost desperate to persuade him. After an uncomfortable silence during which he seemed to be weighing my proposition, he finally spoke: He was willing to discuss the idea further, and perhaps even agree to my request, but only on the condition that he be the first to read the story. And if he didn't like it, he wanted me to bury the pages. I hedged. Writing a book takes months, even years, of effort—but he held firm. In the end, I agreed. Truth be told, I understood his reasoning. If our positions had been reversed, I would have asked the same of him.

We went to the cottage then. I asked questions and received answers. I was provided again with a copy of the story, and I was shown the original drawings and letters that enlivened the past even more.

The conversation rolled on. He told the story well and saved the best for last. As evening fell, he showed me a remarkable item—a labor of love—that enabled me to visualize the events with detail and clarity, as if I'd been a witness to all that had happened. I also began to see how the words would appear on the page, as if the story were writing itself and my role was simply to transcribe it.

Before I left, he requested that real names not be used. He had no desire for fame—he considered himself a private person—but more than that, he knew that the story had the potential to open old, and new, wounds. The events, after all, hadn't taken place in isolation. There were living people involved, some of whom might be upset by the revelations. I have honored his request because I believe that the story has larger value and meaning: the power to remind us that there are times when destiny and love collide.

I began working on the novel soon after that first evening we spent together. In the year that followed, whenever I had questions, I called or visited. I toured the locations, or at least those that hadn't been lost to history. I went through newspaper archives and examined photographs taken more than twenty-five years earlier. To flesh out even more details, I spent a week at a bed and breakfast in a small coastal town in eastern North Carolina and traveled as far as Africa. I was fortunate in that time seems to move more slowly in both of those regions; there were moments when I felt as if I had actually journeyed deep into the past.

My trip to Zimbabwe was especially helpful. I'd never been to that particular country and was over-whelmed by the spectacular wildlife. The country had once been called the breadbasket of Africa, but by the time of my visit, much of the agricultural infrastructure had decayed and the economy had collapsed for largely political reasons. I walked among crumbling farmhouses and fallow fields, dependent on my imagination as to how verdant the land had been when the story first began. I also spent three weeks on various safaris, absorbing everything around me. I spoke to guides and scouts and spotters, discussing their training and their daily lives; I speculated on how challenging it must be for them to maintain families, since they spend most of their time in the bush. I confess, I found Africa utterly seductive. Since those trips, I've often felt the urge to return, and I know I will before long.

In spite of all the research, there's much that remains unknown. Twenty-seven years is a long period of time, and to re-create verbatim an ancient conversation between two people is impossible. Nor is it possible to recall with accuracy each and every step a person takes, or the position of the clouds in the sky, or the rhythm of the waves as they roll up on the shore. What I can say is that what follows next is the best I can possibly do under such constraints. Since I made further alterations for the purposes of privacy, I'm comfortable describing this book as a novel and not a work of nonfiction.

The genesis, research, and creation of this book has been one of the more memorable experiences of my life. In some ways, it's transformed the way I think about love. I suspect that most people harbor a lingering sense of What if I'd followed my heart?, *and there's no way to ever really know the answer. A life, after all, is simply a series of little lives, each of them lived one day at a time, and every single one of those days has choices and consequences. Piece by piece, those decisions help to form the people we become. I've captured some fragments to the best of my ability, but who is to say that the picture I've assembled is a true portrait of who the couple really was?*

There will always be doubters when it comes to love. Falling in love is the easy part; making that love last amid life's varied challenges is an elusive dream for many. But if you read this story with the same sense of wonder that I felt when writing it, then perhaps your faith in the uncanny force that love can exert on people's lives will be renewed. You might even find your way to Kindred Spirit one day, with a story of your own to tell...one that has the power to change someone else's life in ways you never imagined possible.

Nicholas Sparks
September 2, 2017

TRU

On the morning of September 9, 1990, Tru Walls stepped outside and surveyed a morning sky that was the color of fire near the horizon. The earth was cracked beneath his feet and the air was dry; it hadn't rained in more than two months. Dust clung to his boots as he made his way to the pickup he'd owned for more than twenty years. Like his footwear, the truck was covered in dust, both inside and out. Beyond a fence topped with electric wire, an elephant pulled branches from a tree that had toppled earlier that morning. Tru paid it no attention. It was part of the landscape of his birth—his ancestors had emigrated from England more than a century earlier—and he was no more startled than a fisherman spotting a shark as the daily catch was pulled in. He was lean, with dark hair and squint lines at the corners of his eyes earned by a life spent in the sun; at forty-two, he sometimes wondered whether he'd chosen to live in the bush or the bush had chosen him.

The camp was quiet; the other guides—including Romy, his best friend—had left earlier that morning for the main lodge, where they would ferry guests from around the world into the bush. Tru had worked at the lodge in Hwange National Park for the past ten years; prior to that, his existence had been more nomadic, with changes in lodges every couple of years as he'd gained more experience. As a rule, he'd avoided only those lodges that allowed hunting, something his grandfather wouldn't understand. His grandfather—who was referred to by everyone as the Colonel, though he never served in the military—claimed to have killed more than three hundred lions and cheetahs in his lifetime while protecting livestock on the massive family farm near Harare where Tru had been raised; his stepfather and half brothers were steadily making progress toward that same number. In addition to cattle, Tru's family cultivated various crops, harvesting more tobacco and tomatoes than any other farm in the country. Coffee, too. His great-grandfather had worked with the legendary Cecil Rhodes—mining magnate, politician, and emblem of British imperialism—accumulating land, money, and power in the late nineteenth century, before Tru's grandfather took over.

His grandfather, the Colonel, inherited a thriving enterprise from his father, but after World War II, the business expanded exponentially, making the Walls family one of the wealthiest in the country. The Colonel had never understood Tru's desire to escape what was by then a bona fide business empire and life of considerable luxury. Before he'd died—Tru had been twenty-six at the time—he'd once visited a reserve

202 AN EXCERPT FROM EVERY BREATH

where Tru had been working. Though he had slept at the main lodge rather than the guide camp, seeing Tru's living quarters had been a shock to the old man. He'd surveyed a dwelling that he probably regarded as little better than a shack, without insulation or telephones. A kerosene lantern provided lighting, and a small communal generator powered a miniature refrigerator. It was a far cry from the home where Tru had been raised, but the austere surroundings were all Tru needed, especially as evening descended and an ocean of stars appeared overhead. In fact, they were a step up from a few of the previous camps where he'd worked; in two of those, he'd slept in a tent. Here, at least, there was running water and a shower, which he considered something of a luxury, even if they were in a communal bathroom.

On this morning, Tru carried his guitar in its battered case; a lunch box and thermos; a handful of drawings he'd made for his son, Andrew; and a knapsack containing a few days' worth of clothing, toiletries, drawing pads, colored and charcoal pencils, and his passport. Though he'd be gone for about a week, he figured it was all he would need.

His truck was parked beneath a baobab tree. A few of his fellow guides were fond of the dry, pulpy fruit. They'd mix it into their porridge in the morning, but Tru had never developed a taste for it. Tossing his knapsack onto the front seat, he checked the bed of the truck, making sure there was nothing in the back that could be stolen. Though he'd leave the truck at the family farm, there were more than three hundred field workers there, all of whom made very little money.

Good tools were prone to vanishing into the ether, even under the watchful eyes of his family.

He slid behind the wheel and slipped on his sunglasses. Before turning the key, he made sure he hadn't forgotten anything. There wasn't much; in addition to the knapsack and guitar, he carried with him the letter and photograph he'd received from America, along with his plane tickets and his wallet. In the rack behind him was a loaded rifle in case his truck broke down and he found himself wandering in the bush, which remained one of the most dangerous places in the world, especially at night, even for someone as experienced as he. In the glove compartment were a compass and a flashlight. He made sure his tent was beneath the seat, again in case of emergency. It was compact enough to fit in the bed of his truck, and though it wouldn't do much to keep predators at bay, it was better than sleeping on the ground. *All right, then,* he thought. He was as ready as he'd ever be.

The day was already growing warm and the interior of the truck was even hotter. He'd avail himself of the "two-twenty" air-conditioning: two windows down at a speed of twenty miles an hour. It wouldn't help much, but he'd long since grown used to the heat. He rolled up the sleeves of his tan button-up shirt. He wore his usual trekking pants, which had grown soft and comfortable over the years. The guests hanging around the swimming pool back at the main lodge would likely be in bathing suits and flip-flops, but he'd never been comfortable in that attire. The boots and canvas pants had once saved his life when he'd crossed paths with an angry black mamba; if he hadn't had the proper clothing, the venom would have killed him in less than thirty minutes.

He glanced at his watch. It was a little after seven, and he had a long couple of days ahead. Cranking the engine, he backed out before heading toward the gate. He hopped out, pulled the gate open, rolled the truck through, and then closed the gate again. The last thing the other guides needed was to return to camp and find that a pride of lions had settled in. It had happened before—not at this particular camp but at another where he'd worked, in the southeastern part of the country. That had been a chaotic day. No one had been quite sure what to do other than bide their time until the lions figured out how long they intended to stay. Fortunately, the lions had vacated the camp to go on the hunt later in the afternoon, but ever since then, Tru made a point to check the gates, even when he wasn't driving. Some of the guides were new, and he didn't want to take any chances.

Shifting the truck into gear, he settled in, trying to make the ride as smooth as possible. The first hundred miles were on rutted gravel roads pocked with potholes, first on the reserve, then winding past a number of small villages. That part would take until the early afternoon, but he was used to the drive, and he allowed his mind to wander as he took in the world he called home.

The sun glinted through wispy clouds that trailed over the tree line, illuminating a lilac-breasted roller as it broke free from the tree branches on his left. Two warthogs crossed the road ahead of him, trotting past a family of baboons. He'd seen those animals thousands of times, but he still marveled at how they could survive when surrounded by so many predators. Nature had its own insurance policy, he knew. Animals that were low on the food chain had more young; female zebras, for instance, were pregnant for all but nine or ten days a year. It was estimated that female lions, on the other hand, had to mate more than a thousand times for every cub that reached its first birthday. It was evolutionary balance at its finest, and though he witnessed it daily, it still struck him as extraordinary.

Often, guests would ask him about the most exciting things he'd seen while guiding. He'd recount what it was like to be charged by a black rhino, or how he'd once witnessed a giraffe bucking wildly until finally giving birth in an explosive discharge that had surprised him in its violence. He'd seen a jaguar cub dragging a warthog nearly twice its size high into a tree, only inches ahead of a pack of snarling hyenas who'd caught the scent of the kill. One time, he'd followed a wild dog that, abandoned by its own kind, had bonded with a pack of jackals—the same pack it used to hunt. The stories were endless.

Was it possible, he wondered, to experience the same game drive twice? The answer was both yes and no. A person could go to the same lodge, work with the same guide, leave at the same time, and drive the same roads in exactly the same weather in the same season, but always, the animals were in different places, doing different things. They moved to and from watering holes, watching and listening, eating and sleeping and mating, all of them simply trying to survive another day.

Off to the side, he saw a herd of impalas. Guides would joke that those antelopes were the McDonald's of the bush, fast food in abundance. They were part of every predator's diet, and guests usually grew tired of photographing them after a single game drive. Tru, however, slowed the truck, watching as one after another made an impossibly high and graceful leap over a fallen tree, as if choreographed. In their own way, he thought, they were as special as the big five—lion, leopard, rhino, elephant, and water buffalo—or even the big seven, which included cheetahs and hyenas. Those were the animals that guests most wanted to see, the game that inspired the most excitement. The thing was, spotting lions wasn't particularly difficult, at least when the sun was shining. Lions slept eighteen to twenty hours a day, and they could usually be found resting in the shade. Spotting a *moving* lion, on the other hand, was rare, except at night. In the past, he'd worked at lodges that offered evening game drives. A few had been hair-raising, and many had been blinding, the dust from a hundred buffalo or wildebeest or zebra swirling as they'd stampeded from lions. It had been impossible to see more than inches in any direction, forcing Tru to stop the jeep. Twice, he'd realized that his vehicle was suddenly sandwiched between the pride of lions and whatever they'd been hunting, sending his adrenaline skyrocketing.

The road grew steadily rougher, and Tru slowed even more, weaving from one side to the other. He was headed for Bulawayo, the second-largest city in the country and home to his ex-wife, Kim, and their son, Andrew. He had a house there as well, which he'd bought after his divorce. In retrospect, it was obvious that he and Kim hadn't been well suited for each other. They'd met ten years ago at a bar in Harare, when Tru had been between jobs. Later Kim would tell him that he'd struck her as exotic, which along with his last name was enough to pique her interest. As for her, she was eight years younger and beautiful, with an easygoing yet confident charm. One thing led to the next, and they'd ended up spending much of the next six weeks together. By then, the bush was calling to Tru again and he'd wanted to end the relationship; instead, she'd told him she was pregnant. They got married, Tru took a job at Hwange because of its relative proximity to Bulawayo, and Andrew came along not long after that.

Though she'd known what Tru did for a living, Kim had assumed that when they had a child, Tru would find a job that didn't keep him away for weeks on end. Instead, he continued to guide, Kim eventually met someone else, and their marriage came to an end less than five years after it had started. There were no hard feelings on either side; if anything, their relationship had improved since their divorce. Whenever he picked up Andrew, he and Kim would visit for a while, catching up like the old friends they were. She'd remarried and had a daughter with her second husband, Ken; on their last visit, she'd told Tru she was pregnant again. Ken worked in the finance office of Air Zimbabwe. He wore a suit to work and was home every night for dinner. That's what Kim wanted, and Tru was happy for her.

As for Andrew...

His son was ten now, and the one great thing to come out of the marriage. As fate would have it, Tru contracted the measles when Andrew was a few months old, leaving him sterile, but he had never felt the need for another child. For him, Andrew had always been more than enough, and he was the reason Tru was detouring to Bulawayo instead of heading straight to the farm. With blond hair and brown eyes, Andrew resembled his mother, and Tru had dozens of drawings of him tacked to the walls of his shack. Over the years, he'd added photographs—on almost every visit, Kim would hand Tru an envelope filled with them—different versions of his son blending together, evolving into someone entirely new. At least once a week, Tru would sketch something he'd seen in the bush—usually an animal—but other times, he would draw the two of them, trying to capture a memory from their previous visit.

Balancing family and work had been a challenge, especially after the divorce. For six weeks, while he worked at the camp, Kim had custody and Tru would be entirely absent from his son's life: no calls, no visits, no impromptu soccer matches or ice cream runs. Then, for two weeks, Tru would assume custody and play the role of full-time father. Andrew would stay with him in his house in Bulawayo, Tru ferrying him to and from school, packing lunches and making dinner, and helping with homework. On the weekends, they did whatever Andrew chose, and in each and every one of those moments, Tru would wonder how it was possible to love his son as deeply as he did, even if he wasn't always around to show it.

Off to the right, he spotted a pair of circling buzzards. Searching for something left over from the hyenas last night, perhaps, or maybe looking for an animal that had died earlier in the morning. Lately, many of the animals had been struggling. The country was in the midst of yet another drought, and the watering holes in this area of the reserve had gone dry. It wasn't surprising; not far to the west, in Botswana, lay the vast Kalahari Desert, home of the legendary San people. Their language was thought to be one of the oldest in existence, heavy on knocks and clicks, and sounded almost alien to outsiders. Despite having virtually nothing in the way of material things, they joked and laughed more than any other group of people he'd ever met, but he wondered how long they would be able to maintain their way of life. Modernity was encroaching and there were rumors that the government of Botswana was going to require that all children in the country be educated in schools, including the San. He guessed that would eventually spell the end of a culture that had existed for thousands of years.

But Africa was always changing. He'd been born in Rhodesia, a colony of the British Empire; he'd watched the country descend into civil unrest, and he had still been a teenager when the country finally split, eventually becoming the nations of Zimbabwe and Zambia. Like in South Africa—which was regarded as a pariah because of apartheid in much of the civilized world—in Zimbabwe, much of the wealth was concentrated among a tiny percentage of the population, almost all of them white. Tru doubted that would last forever, but politics and social inequality were subjects he no longer discussed with his family. They were, after all, part of that privileged group, and like all privileged groups, they believed they deserved their riches and advantages, no matter how brutally the original wealth and power might have been accrued.

Tru eventually reached the limits of the reserve and passed the first of the small villages, home to about a hundred people. Like the guide camp, the village was fenced for the safety of both the people and the animals. He reached for his thermos and took a drink, resting his elbow on the windowsill. He passed a woman on a bicycle loaded down with boxes of vegetables, then a man who was walking, most likely headed for the next village, about six miles away. Tru slowed and pulled over; the man ambled to the truck and got in. Tru spoke enough of the man's language to keep a conversation going; in all, he was relatively fluent in six languages, two of them tribal. The other four were English, French, German, and Spanish. It was one of the qualities that made him an employee sought after by lodges.

He eventually dropped the man off and continued his drive, finally reaching a road paved in asphalt. He stopped for lunch soon after, simply pulling off the road to eat in the bed of his truck in the shade of an acacia tree. The sun was high by then and the world around him was quiet, no animals in sight.

Back on the road after lunch, he made better time. The villages eventually gave way to smaller towns, then larger ones, and late in the afternoon, he reached the outskirts of Bulawayo. He'd written Kim a letter, telling her when he'd be arriving, but mail in Zimbabwe wasn't always predictable. Letters usually reached their destination, but timeliness wasn't something that could be counted on.

Pulling onto her street, he parked behind Kim's car in the driveway. He approached the door and knocked; moments later, she answered, clearly expecting him. As they hugged, Tru heard his son's voice. Andrew tumbled down the stairs, leaping into Tru's arms. Tru knew that the time would come when Andrew considered himself too old for such displays of affection, so he squeezed tighter, wondering whether any joy could ever surpass this.

"Mummy told me that you're going to America," Andrew said to him later that night. They were sitting out front, on a low wall that served as a fence between Kim's house and the neighbor's.

"I am. But I'm not staying long. I'll be back next week."

"I wish you didn't have to go."

Tru slipped his arm around his son. "I know. I'll miss you, too."

"Then why are you going?"

That was the question, wasn't it? Why, after all this time, had the letter arrived? Along with a plane ticket?

"I'm going to see my father," Tru finally answered.

Andrew squinted, his blond hair bright in the moonlight. "You mean Papa Rodney?"

"No," Tru said. "I'm going to see my biological father. I've never met him."

"Do you want to meet him?"

Yes, Tru thought, then, *No, not really.* "I don't know," he finally admitted.

"Then why are you going?"

"Because," Tru said, "in his letter, he told me that he was dying."

After saying goodbye to Andrew, Tru drove to his house. Once inside, he opened the windows to air the place out, unpacked his guitar, and played and sang for an hour before finally turning in for the night.

He was out the door early the following morning. Unlike those in the park, the roads to the capital city were relatively well maintained, but it still took most of the day to get there. Tru arrived after dark to see lights shining in the stately home that his stepfather, Rodney, had rebuilt after the fire. Nearby were three other houses—one for each of his half brothers and the even larger main house where the Colonel had once lived. Technically, Tru owned the main house, but he made his way toward a smaller shack structure near the fence line. In the distant past, the bungalow had once housed the chef and his wife; Tru had fixed up the place in his early teen years. While he'd still been alive, the Colonel had seen that the bungalow was cleaned somewhat regularly, but that no longer happened. There was dust everywhere, and Tru had to shake the spiders and beetles from the sheets before crawling into bed. It mattered little to him; he'd slept in worse conditions countless times.

In the morning, he avoided his family. Instead, he had Tengwe, the crew foreman, drive him to the airport. Tengwe was gray haired and wiry and knew how to coax life out of the ground in the harshest conditions imaginable. His six children worked at the farm, and his wife, Anoona, prepared meals for Rodney. After his mother's death, Tru had been closer to Tengwe and Anoona than even the Colonel, and they were the only ones at the farm he ever missed.

The roads in Harare were clogged with cars and trucks, carts and bikes and pedestrians; the airport was even more chaotic. After checking in, Tru boarded a flight that would take him first to Amsterdam, then to New York and Charlotte, and finally to Wilmington, North Carolina.

With layovers, he was in transit for nearly twenty-one hours before he stepped onto U.S. soil for the first time in his life. When he reached the baggage claim area in Wilmington, he spotted a man holding a sign with his name on it, above the name of a limousine service. The driver was surprised by the lack of checked luggage and offered to carry both the guitar case and the knapsack. Tru shook his head. Stepping outside, he could feel his shirt beginning to tack to his back in the thick, humid air as they trudged to the car.

The drive was uneventful, but the world beyond the car windows was foreign to him. The landscape, flat and lush and verdant, seemed to stretch in every direction; he saw palms intermingled with oaks and pine trees, and grass the color of emeralds. Wilmington was a small, low-lying city featuring a mix of chain stores and local businesses that eventually gave way to a historic area with homes that looked at least a couple of hundred years old. His driver pointed out the Cape Fear River, its brackish waters dotted with fishing boats. On the roads, he saw cars and SUVs and mini-vans, none of them straddling the lanes as they did in Bulawayo, avoiding carts and animals. No one was riding a bicycle or walking, and nearly every person he saw on the city sidewalks was white. The world he'd left behind felt as distant as a dream.

An hour later, Tru crossed a floating pontoon bridge and was dropped off at a three-story home nestled against a low-rising dune in a place called Sunset Beach, an island just off the coast near the South Carolina border. It took him a moment to understand that the entire bottom floor was comprised of garages; the whole structure seemed almost grotesque compared to the much smaller house next door, which displayed a FOR SALE sign out front. He wondered whether the driver had made a mistake, but the driver checked the address again and assured him that he was in the right place. As the car pulled away, he heard the deep, rhythmic pulsation of ocean waves rolling ashore. He tried to remember the last time he'd heard that sound. A decade at least, Tru guessed as he climbed the steps to the second floor.

The driver had given him an envelope containing the key to the front door, and he stepped past the foyer into an expansive great room with pine flooring and a wood-beamed ceiling. The beach house decor looked like something staged for a magazine, every throw pillow and blanket placed with tasteful precision. Large windows offered a view of the back deck and an expanse of sea grass and dunes beyond, stretching to the ocean. A spacious dining area extended off the great room, and the designer kitchen included custom cabinetry, marble countertops, and premium appliances.

A note on the counter informed him that the refrigerator and pantry had been stocked with food and drinks, and that if he needed to go anywhere, he could call the limousine company. Should he be interested in ocean activities, a surfboard and fishing gear could be found in the garage. According to the note, Tru's father hoped to arrive on Saturday afternoon. He apologized that he wasn't able to get there sooner, although no explanation was offered for the delay. As he set the note aside, Tru was struck by the idea that perhaps his father was as ambivalent about their meeting as Tru was...which raised the question as to why he'd provided the airline ticket in the first place. Well, Tru would soon find out.

It was Tuesday evening, so Tru would have a few days to himself. He hadn't anticipated that, but there wasn't much he could do at this point. He spent the next few minutes exploring the house, learning the layout. The master bedroom was down the hall from the kitchen, and it was there that he left his belongings. Upstairs, there were additional bedrooms and bathrooms, all of which appeared pristine and unused. In the master bathroom he found fresh towels along with soap, shampoo, and conditioner, and he treated himself to an extra-long shower, lingering beneath the spray.

His hair was still damp as he stepped onto the back deck. The air remained warm, but the sun was sinking lower and the sky had fanned into a thousand shades of yellow and orange. Squinting into the distance, he could just make out what looked to be a pod of porpoises playing in the waves beyond the breakers. A latched gate gave way to steps that descended to a planked walkway over the grasses; following the steps, he trekked out to the final dune, discovering more steps leading to the beach.

There were few people about. In the distance, he saw a woman trailing behind a small dog; in the opposite direction, a few surfers floated on their boards near a pier that stretched into the ocean like a pointed finger. He started toward the pier, walking on the compact sand near the water's edge, musing that until recently, he'd never heard of Sunset Beach. He wasn't sure he'd ever thought about North Carolina at all. He tried to recall whether any of his guests over the years had come from here, without luck. He supposed it didn't make any difference.

At the pier, he took the stairs up and strolled to the end. Resting his arms on the railings, he gazed over water that stretched to the horizon. The sight of it, the immensity of it, was almost beyond comprehension. It reminded him that there was an entire world out there to explore, and he wondered if he would ever get around to doing it. Maybe when Andrew was older, they'd spend some time traveling together...

As the breeze picked up, the moon began its slow ascent into an indigo sky. He took it as a cue to head back. He assumed his father owned the place. It might have been a rental, but the furnishings were too pricey to trust to strangers, and besides, if that was the case, why not simply put Tru up at a hotel? He wondered again about the delay until Saturday. Why had he flown Tru out so far in advance? If the man was indeed dying, Tru speculated that it could be something medical, which meant there was no guarantee about Saturday, either.

But what would happen when his father did show up? The man was a stranger; a single meeting wasn't going to change that. Nonetheless, Tru hoped he'd be able to answer some questions, which was the only reason Tru had decided to come in the first place.

Entering the house, he fished out a steak from the refrigerator. He had to open a few of the cabinets before he found a cast-iron fry pan, but the stove, as fancy as it was, functioned similarly to the ones back home. There were also various food items from a place called Murray's Deli, and he added what appeared to be some kind of cabbage salad as well as potato salad to his plate. After he ate, he washed the plate, glass, and utensils by hand and grabbed his guitar before returning to the back deck. He played and sang softly to himself for an hour while the occasional shooting star passed overhead. He thought about Andrew and Kim, his mother and grandfather, before finally becoming sleepy enough to go to bed.

In the morning, he did a hundred push-ups and a hundred sit-ups before trying and failing to make some coffee. He couldn't figure out how the machine worked. Too many buttons, too many options, and he had no idea where to add the water. He decided to visit the beach instead, hoping to stumble upon a place to buy a cup.

Like the evening before, he had the beach mostly to himself. He thought about how pleasant it was to spontaneously take a walk. He couldn't do that at Hwange, not without a rifle, anyway. He breathed deeply when he reached the sand, tasting salt in the air, feeling like the foreigner he was.

He slipped his hands into his pockets, taking in the morning. He had been walking for fifteen minutes when he spotted a cat crouched on top of a dune, next to a deck that was under repair, the steps to the beach still unfinished. At the farm, there had been barn cats, but this one looked as though it spent most of its time indoors. Just then, a small white dog raced past him, barreling toward a flock of seagulls that burst into the air like a small explosion. The dog eventually veered toward the dune, spotted the cat, and took off like a rocket. The cat jumped up to the deck as the dog scrambled up the dune in pursuit, both of them vanishing from sight. A minute later, he thought he heard the distant screech of car tires, followed by the sound of a dog yelping and crying.

He glanced behind him; halfway down the beach, he saw a woman standing near the water, no doubt the dog's owner, her gaze fixed on the ocean. He guessed she was the same woman he'd spotted the night before, but she was too far away to have seen or heard what had happened.

Hesitating briefly, Tru started after the dog, his feet slipping in the sand as he scaled the dune. Stepping onto the deck, he followed the walkway, eventually reaching a new set of steps leading on one side up to the house's deck and on the other, down to the ground. He went down, winding between two houses that were similar in style to the one where he was staying. Climbing over a low retaining wall, he continued to the road. No car in sight. No hysterical people or dog lying in the road, either. That was good news, as an initial matter. He knew from experience that wounded animals often sought shelter if they were still able to move, nature's way of allowing them to heal while hiding from predators.

He walked along one side of the road, searching the bushes and around trees. He didn't see anything. Crossing the street, he repeated the process and eventually came across the dog standing near a hedge, its rear leg bobbing up and down. The dog was panting and shaking, whether from pain or shock, Tru couldn't tell. He debated whether to go back to the beach and try to find the woman, but he was afraid the dog might hobble away to parts unknown. Removing his sunglasses, he squatted down and held his hand out.

"Hey there," he said, keeping his voice calm and steady, "You all right?"

The dog tilted its head and Tru slowly began to inch toward it, speaking in low, steady tones. When Tru was close, the dog stretched out, trying to sniff his hand, before taking a couple of hesitant steps forward. When the dog finally seemed convinced of his good intentions, it relaxed. Tru stroked its head and checked for blood. Nothing. On its collar tag, Tru saw the name *Scottie*.

"Hi, Scottie," he said. "Let's get you back to the beach, shall we? Come on."

It took some coaxing, but Scottie finally began to follow Tru back toward the dune. He was limping, but not to the point where Tru thought anything might be broken. When Scottie stopped at the retaining wall, Tru hesitated before finally reaching down and scooping him into his arms. He carried him between the houses and up the steps to the walkway, then eventually over the dune. Scanning the beach, he spotted the woman, much nearer now.

Tru eased down the dune and started toward her. The morning remained bright, but the woman seemed even brighter, amplified by the sunny yellow fabric of her sleeveless top fluttering in the wind. He watched as the gap between them continued to close, studying her as she drew near. Despite the confusion on her face, she was beautiful, with untamed auburn hair and eyes the color of turquoise. And almost at once, something inside him began to stir, something that made him feel a bit nervous, the way he always felt in the presence of an attractive woman.

HOPE

Hope stepped from the back deck to the walkway that led over the dune, trying to keep her coffee from spilling. Scottie—her aptly named Scottish terrier—strained at the leash, eager to reach the beach.

"Stop pulling," she said.

The dog ignored her. Scottie had been a gift from Josh, her boyfriend of the past six years, and he barely listened on his best days. But since arriving at the cottage the day before, he'd been positively wild. His paws scuffled madly against the sandy steps as they descended to the beach, and she reminded herself that she needed to bring him to another one of those weekend obedience training programs, though she doubted it would do any good. He'd flunked out of the first two already. Scottie—the sweetest and cutest dog in the world—seemed to be a bit of a dim bulb, bless his heart. Then again, maybe he was just stubborn.

Because Labor Day had come and gone, the beach was quiet, most of the elegant homes dark. She saw someone jogging near the pier; in the opposite direction, a couple strolled near the water. She leaned over, setting the foam cup in the sand while she released Scottie from the leash, watching as her dog sprinted away. She doubted anyone would care. Last night, she'd seen two other dogs off leash, and in any case there weren't too many people around to complain.

Hope started walking and took a sip of her coffee. She hadn't slept well. Usually, the endless roar of the waves lulled her immediately to sleep, but not last night. She'd tossed and turned, woken multiple times, and had finally given up for good when sunlight began streaming into her room.

At least the weather was perfect, with blue skies and a temperature more typical of early autumn than late summer. On the news last night, they had predicted storms over the weekend, and her friend Ellen was crazy with worry. Ellen was getting married on Saturday, and both the wedding and the reception were supposed to be outdoors at the Wilmington Country Club, somewhere near the eighteenth green. Hope figured there was probably a backup plan—no doubt, they'd be able to use the clubhouse—but when Ellen had called last night, she'd nearly been in tears.

Hope had been sympathetic on the phone, but it hadn't been easy. Ellen was so caught up in her own worries that she hadn't so much as asked how Hope was doing. In a way, that was probably a good thing; the last thing Hope wanted to talk about right now was Josh. How was she supposed to explain that Josh was going to be a no-show for the wedding? Or that—as disappointing as a rained-out wedding could be—there were definitely worse things?

Right now, Hope was feeling a bit overwhelmed by life in general, and spending the week alone at the cottage wasn't helping. Not only because Josh wasn't around, but because it was probably the last week she'd ever spend here. Her parents had listed the cottage with a Realtor earlier in the summer, and they'd accepted an offer ten days ago. She understood why they were selling, but she was going to miss this place. Growing up, most of her summers and holidays had been spent here, and every nook and cranny held memories. She could recall washing the sand from her feet with the garden hose, watching storms from the window seat in the kitchen, and the scent of fish or steaks being grilled on the barbecue on the back deck. She remembered swapping late-night secrets with her sisters in their shared room, and it was here that she'd kissed a boy for the very first time. She had been twelve years old and his name was Tony; for years, his family had owned the cottage three doors down. She'd had a crush on him most of the summer, and after they'd split a peanut butter and jelly sandwich, he'd kissed her in the kitchen while her mom had been watering plants on the deck.

The memory still made her smile, and she wondered what the new owners intended to do with the place. She wanted to imagine that they wouldn't change a thing, but she wasn't naive. During her childhood, the cottage had been one of many similarly sized homes along this stretch of shoreline; now there were only a few cottages remaining. In recent years, Sunset Beach had been discovered by the wealthy, and more than likely, the cottage would be razed and a new, much larger home constructed, like the three-story monstrosity right next door. It was the way of the world, she supposed, but it nonetheless felt like part of her was being razed as well. She knew it was crazy thinking—a little too *woe is me*—and she chided herself for it. Playing the martyr wasn't like her; until recently, she'd always thought of herself as a glass-half-full, *because today is a new day* kind of girl. And why not? In most ways her life *had* been blessed. She had loving parents and two wonderful older sisters; she was an aunt to three boys and two girls, who were a source of constant joy and surprise to her. She'd done well in school, and she enjoyed her work as a trauma nurse in the ER at Wake County Medical Center. Despite the few pounds she wanted to lose, she was healthy. She and Josh—an orthopedic surgeon—had been dating since she was thirty, and she loved him. She had good friends and owned her own condominium in Raleigh, not far from her parents. From the outside, everything looked just peachy.

So why was she feeling so wonky right now?

Because it was one more trying thing in an already trying year, beginning first and foremost with her dad's diagnosis, that particular soul-crushing bombshell arriving in April. Her dad was the only one who hadn't been surprised at the news from the doctor. He'd known something was amiss when he no longer had the energy to jog in the woods behind his house.

Her dad had exercised in those woods for as long as she could remember; despite the construction engulfing Raleigh, the area had been designated a greenbelt, which was one of the reasons her parents had bought their home in the first place. Over the years, various developers had tried to overturn the city's decision, promising jobs and tax revenue; they did so without success, partly because her father had opposed them at every meeting of the city council.

Her dad adored the woods. Not only did he run there in the mornings, but after he finished at the school, he would walk the paths he'd followed earlier in the morning. When she was a little girl, she would tag along with him after work, chasing butterflies or tossing sticks, hunting for crawdads in the small creek that wove toward the path in places. Her dad was a high school science teacher who knew the names of every bush and tree they passed. He would point out the differences between a southern red oak and a black oak and in that instant, the distinctions were as obvious as the color of the sky. Later, though, if she attempted it on her own, the information jumbled together. The same thing would happen when they stared at constellations in the sky; he'd point out Hercules, Lyra, or Aquila and she'd nod in wonder, only to squint in confusion at the same sky a week later, trying to remember which one was which.

For a long time, she'd believed her dad to be the smartest man in the world. When she would tell him that, he'd always laugh and say that if that were true, then he would have figured out a way to earn a million dollars. Her mom was a teacher, too—second grade—and it wasn't until Hope graduated from college and began paying her own bills that she realized how much of a financial challenge it must have been for them to raise a family, even on their combined income.

Her dad had been a coach to the high school's cross country and track teams as well. He never raised his voice, but nonetheless led his teams to numerous conference championships. Along with her sisters, Hope had participated in both sports all four years of high school, and though none of them were stars, Hope still jogged a few times a week. Her older sisters ran three or four days a week, and for the past ten years, Hope had joined her dad and her sisters at the annual Turkey Trot on Thanksgiving morning, all of them working up an appetite before sitting down at the table. Two years earlier, her dad had won his age-group bracket.

But now, her dad would never run again.

It had started with occasional twitches and a slight, if noticeable, fatigue. For how long, she wasn't exactly sure, but she guessed that it had been a couple of years. In the twelve months after that, the runs in the woods became jogs, and then finally walks.

Old age, his internist suggested, and it made sense. By then, her dad was in his late sixties—he'd retired four years earlier—and he had arthritis in his hips and feet. Despite a life of exercise, he took medication for slightly elevated blood pressure. Then, last January, he'd caught a cold. It was a normal, run-of-the-mill cold, but after a few weeks, her dad had still found it harder to breathe than usual.

Hope had gone with him to another appointment with his internist. More tests were done. Blood work was sent to the labs. He was referred to another doctor, then another. A muscle biopsy was taken, and when the results came back, there was the suggestion of a potential neurological problem. It was at that point that Hope began to worry.

More tests followed, and later, Hope sat with the rest of her family as the diagnosis of amyotrophic lateral sclerosis was pronounced. Lou Gehrig's disease, the same disease that put Stephen Hawking in a wheelchair, caused the death of neurons that control voluntary muscles, the doctor explained. Muscles gradually weakened, resulting in loss of mobility, swallowing, and speaking. And, then, finally, breathing. There was no known cure.

Nor was there any way to predict how quickly the disease would progress. In the months since the diagnosis, her father had seemed little changed, physically. He still went for his walks in the woods, still had the same gentle spirit and unwavering faith in God, still held hands with her mom as the two of them sat on the couch and watched television in the evenings. That gave her hope that he had a slow-progressing version of the disease, but she worried all the time. How long would her dad remain mobile? How long would her mom be able to handle his care without help? Should they start building ramps and add a railing for the shower? Knowing there were wait lists for the best places, should they start researching assisted-living facilities? And how would they ever pay for it? Her parents were anything but wealthy. They had their pensions and small savings, and they owned their home and the beach cottage, but that was it. Would that be enough, not only for her father's medical care but for her mom's remaining years as well? And if not, what would they do?

Too many questions, with little in the way of answers. Her mom and dad seemed to accept the uncertainty, as did her sisters, but Hope had always been more of a planner. She was the kind of person who would lie awake at night anticipating various possibilities and making hypothetical decisions about pretty much everything. It made her feel like she was somehow better prepared for whatever might come, but on the downside, it led to a life that sometimes cascaded from one worry to the next. Which was exactly what happened whenever she thought about her dad.

But he was doing okay, she reminded herself. And he might be okay three or five or even ten years from now; there was no way to tell. Two days ago, before she'd left for the beach, they'd even gone on a walk, just like they used to. Granted, it was slower and shorter than their walks had been in the past, but her dad could still name all the trees and bushes, and he shared his knowledge one more time. As they were walking, he'd stopped and leaned over, lifting a fallen leaf that presaged the arrival of autumn.

"One of the great things about a leaf," he said to her, "is that it reminds you to live as well as you can for as long as you can, until it's finally time to let go and allow yourself to drift away with grace."

She liked what her dad had told her. Well... *kind of.* No doubt he'd viewed the fallen leaf as a teachable moment, and she knew there was both truth and value in what he said, but was it really possible to face death without any fear at all? To gracefully drift away?

If anyone could do it, her dad probably could. He was just about the most even-keeled, balanced, and peaceful person she'd ever met, which was probably one of the reasons he'd been married to her mom for fifty years and still liked to hold her hand and smooch when he thought the girls weren't paying attention. She often wondered how the two of them could make being in love seem both intentional and effortless at the same time.

That had left her in a funk, too. Well, not so much because of her mom and dad, but because of Josh. As much as she loved him, she'd never gotten used to the on-again, off-again nature of their relationship. Right now they were in the off-again position, which was the reason that Hope was spending the week at the cottage alone except for Scottie, with only a pedicure and time with the hairstylist on the agenda until the rehearsal dinner on Friday night.

Josh was supposed to have come with her this week, and as the date of the trip had approached, Hope had become ever more certain they needed some time alone together. For the last nine months, the practice where he worked had been trying to hire two more orthopedic surgeons to handle the surging patient load, without luck. Which meant Josh had been working seventy- to eighty-hour weeks, and had been on call constantly. Even worse, his days off weren't always in sync with hers, and lately, he seemed to feel a greater-than-usual need to blow off steam in his own way. On his few free weekends, he tended to prefer hanging out with his buddies, boating or water-skiing or overnighting in Charlotte after hitting the bars, instead of spending time with her.

It wasn't the first time that Josh had drifted into a phase like this one, where Hope sometimes felt like an afterthought. He'd never been the type who sent flowers, and the tender gestures her parents shared every day probably seemed utterly foreign to him. There was also, especially at times like these, a bit of Peter Pan about him, a quality that made her wonder whether he would ever really grow up. His apartment, filled with IKEA furniture, baseball pennants, and movie posters, seemed more suitable for a graduate student, which made sense, since he hadn't moved since he'd started medical school. His friends—most of whom he'd met at the gym—were in their late twenties or early thirties, single, and as handsome as Josh was. Josh didn't look his age—he'd be forty in a few months—but for the life of her, she couldn't understand how hanging out at bars with his buddies, who were most likely there to meet women, was something he would still find appealing. But what was she supposed to say to him? "Don't hang out with your friends"? She and Josh weren't married, they weren't even engaged, and he'd told her all along that what he wanted in a partner was someone who wouldn't try to change him. He wanted to be accepted for who he was.

She understood that. She wanted to be accepted for who she was, too. So why did it matter if he liked to hang out with his buddies at bars?

Because, she heard a voice inside her answer, *right now we're not technically together and anything is possible. He hasn't always been faithful during previous breakups, has he?*

Oh yeah. *That*. It had happened when they'd broken up the second and third times. Josh had come clean both times and told her what had occurred—women who'd meant nothing to him, terrible mistakes—and he'd sworn it would never happen again. They'd been able to move past it, she'd thought, but...now they were broken up again, and she could feel those old fears cropping up. Even worse, Josh and his friends were in Las Vegas, no doubt living it up and doing whatever it was that guys did while they were there. She wasn't sure exactly what a guys' weekend in Las Vegas might entail, but strip clubs came immediately to mind. She strongly doubted that any of them were lining up to see Siegfried and Roy. Las Vegas was nicknamed Sin City for a reason.

The whole situation still irritated her. Not only because he'd abandoned her this week, but because breaking up, even temporarily, had been so unnecessary in the first place. Couples argued. *That's what they did.* And then afterward, they discussed the situation, learned from their mistakes, tried to forgive, and moved on from there. But Josh didn't seem to understand that notion, and it left her questioning whether the two of them still had a future.

Sometimes she asked herself why she still wanted him in her life, but deep down, she knew the answer. As furious as she was with him and as frustrating as she found some of his ingrained traits, he was whip-smart and handsome enough to make her heart lurch. Even after all these years, Hope could still get lost in his dark violet eyes. Despite his weekends with the guys, she knew he loved her; a few years earlier, when Hope had been in a car accident, Josh had raced immediately from work and refused to leave her hospital bedside for two straight days. When her dad needed referrals to a neurologist, Josh had taken control of that situation, earning the gratitude of her entire family. He looked after her in little ways, taking her car in for oil changes or to rotate her tires, and every once in a while he would surprise her with a home-cooked dinner. At family gatherings and with her friends, Josh remembered details of everyone's lives and had a gracious knack for making them feel at ease.

They also shared the same interests. They both enjoyed hiking and concerts and had the same taste in music; in the past six years, they'd traveled to New York City, Chicago, Cancun, and the Bahamas, and every one of those getaways had validated her reasons for being with him. When life with Josh was good, it felt like everything she wanted, forever. But when it wasn't good, she admitted, it was terrible. She suspected there might be something addictive about those dramatic ups and downs, but she had no way to know for sure. All she knew was that as unbearable as life with him sometimes felt, she couldn't quite imagine life without him, either.

Up ahead, Scottie was trotting and sniffing, weaving toward terns and sending them into deeper water. Changing directions, he raced for the dune for no reason that Hope could deduce. When they got back to the cottage, he'd probably spend the rest of the morning comatose with exhaustion. Thank God for small favors.

She took another sip of coffee, wishing things were different. Her parents made marriage seem effortless; her sisters were cut from the same cloth. Even her friends seemed to float along in their relationships while she and Josh were either soaring or sinking. And why had her most recent argument with Josh been their worst ever?

Thinking back, she suspected that she had been as much to blame as he was. He was stressed about work, and she was admittedly stressed about...well, their future, actually. But instead of finding solace in each other's company, they had let the stress slowly amplify over a period of months until it finally blew. She couldn't even remember how the argument had started other than that she'd mentioned Ellen's upcoming wedding, and Josh had grown quiet. It was clear he was upset about something, but when she asked what was wrong, Josh told her it was nothing.

Nothing.

She hated that word. It was a way to end conversations, not begin them, and maybe she shouldn't have pressed him about it. But she had, and for whatever reason, what had originally begun as the mere mention of a friend's wedding turned into shouts and screams, and the next thing she knew, Josh was storming out the door to spend the night at his brother's house. The following day, he'd told Hope that he thought they needed to take a break to evaluate things, and a few days after that, he'd texted to say that he and his buddies were heading to Las Vegas the week of the wedding.

That had been almost a month ago. They'd talked on the phone a few times since then, but those calls had done little to soothe her, and he hadn't called at all in nearly a week. She wished she could roll back the clock and start over, but what she really wanted was for Josh to feel the same way. And for him to apologize. His reaction to the argument had been so over-the-top; it felt as though it hadn't been enough to sink the knife in her heart; he'd needed to twist it as well. Things like that didn't bode well in the long run, but would he ever change? And if not, where did that leave her? She was thirty-six years old, unmarried, and the last thing she wanted was to start over in the dating scene. She couldn't even imagine it. What was she supposed to do—hang out at bars while guys like Josh's friends hit on her? No, thank you. Besides, she'd devoted six years to Josh; she didn't want to believe that it had been a waste of time. As crazy as he could sometimes make her feel, he had so many good qualities...

She finished her coffee. Up ahead, she saw a man walking near the water's edge. Scottie raced past him, closing fast on another flock of seagulls. She tried to immerse herself in the ocean view, watching the ripples shift from yellow to gold in the morning light. The waves were mild and the sea was calm; her dad would tell her that it likely meant a storm was coming, but Hope decided not to mention that to Ellen if her friend called again. Ellen wouldn't want to hear it.

Hope ran a hand through her hair, tucking loose strands behind her ear. There were wispy clouds on the horizon, the kind that would likely burn off as the morning progressed. It would be a perfect afternoon for a glass of wine, maybe some cheese and crackers, or even oysters on the half shell. Add some candles and some sultry R&B, and...

Why was she thinking such things?

With a sigh, she focused on the waves, recalling that as a little girl, she used to play in them for hours. Sometimes she rode a boogie board, other times it was fun diving under them as they broke overhead. More often than not, her dad would join her in the water for a while, and the memories brought with them a tinge of sadness.

Soon, she thought, her dad would never enter the ocean again.

Staring out over the water, Hope reminded herself that she was fretting over first-world problems. It wasn't as though she were worrying about whether she'd eat today, or have a safe place to sleep. The water she drank didn't heighten her risk of contracting cholera or dysentery; she had clothing, and an education, and the list went on and on and on.

Her dad—what with his leaf story and all—wouldn't want her to worry about him. And as for Josh, more than likely, he'd come around. Of their four previous break-ups, none had lasted longer than six weeks, and in each case, it had been Josh who'd suggested that they start over. As for Hope, she was a big believer in the philosophy *If you love something, set it free, and if it comes back it loves you.* Common sense told her that begging someone to stay was often the same as begging someone to love you, and she was wise enough to know that never worked.

Turning from the water, she began to meander down the beach again. Shading her eyes, she searched for

Scottie up ahead but couldn't find him. She scanned the area behind her, wondering how he could have slipped past her, but he wasn't there, either. Other than her, the beach was empty, and she felt the first twinge of worry. On previous walks, it had sometimes taken her a few seconds to locate him, but he wasn't the kind of dog that would simply run off. It occurred to her that he might have chased some birds into the water and gotten caught in an undertow, but Scottie never swam in the ocean. And yet, he was...gone.

It was then that she spotted someone walking over the dune a short distance up the beach. Her dad still would have made a big deal about that. Dunes were fragile and people were supposed to use the public access paths if there were no steps to the beach, but... whatever. She had more immediate concerns...

She peered ahead and behind, her gaze returning to the man. He'd reached the beach, and she thought she'd ask him whether he'd seen Scottie. It was doubtful, but she didn't know what else to do. Veering in his direction, she absently noticed that he seemed to be carrying something. Whatever it was blended in with the white shirt he was wearing, and it took her a moment to realize that he had Scottie in his arms. She picked up her pace.

The man walked toward her, moving with an almost animal-like grace. He was dressed in faded jeans and a white button-up shirt, the sleeves rolled to the elbows. As he approached, she noticed his shirt was unbuttoned at the top, revealing chest muscles that indicated both exercise and an active life. He had dark blue eyes, like the sky in late afternoon, and coal-black hair that was turning gray near his ears. When he offered a sheepish smile, she noted the dimple on his chin and an unexpected familiarity in his expression, one that strangely made her feel as if they'd known each other all their lives.